NIGHTMARE ON THE NILE

Roger and Veronica Stewart believed that a trip to Egypt would make their honeymoon into the holiday of a lifetime. But the dark influence of Middle Eastern intrigue ensnared them in its web. Fate gave them possession of a roll of undeveloped film, which was vital to several people; among them the Israeli Shabetai, and Major Faizal Hassain of the Egyptian security police. The Stewarts' honeymoon became a nightmare, with death along both banks of the Nile.

Books by Charles Leader
in the Linford Mystery Library:

A WREATH OF POPPIES
A WREATH FOR MISS WONG
A WREATH FROM BANGKOK
A WREATH OF CHERRY BLOSSOM
THE DOUBLE M MAN
KINGDOM OF DARKNESS
DEATH OF A MARINE
SALESMAN OF DEATH
SCAVENGERS OF WAR
THE DRAGON ROARS
THE GOLDEN LURE
CARGO TO SAIGON
STRANGLER'S MOON
FRONTIER OF VIOLENCE
MURDER IN MARRAKECH

CHARLES LEADER

NIGHTMARE ON THE NILE

Complete and Unabridged

LINFORD
Leicester

First published in Great Britain

First Linford Edition
published 1998

British Library CIP Data

Leader, Charles, *1938*–
Nightmare on the Nile.—Large print ed.—
Linford mystery library
1. Detective and mystery stories
2. Large type books
I. Title
823.9′14 [F]

ISBN 0–7089–5296–8

Published by
F. A. Thorpe (Publishing) Ltd.
Anstey, Leicestershire

Set by Words & Graphics Ltd.
Anstey, Leicestershire
Printed and bound in Great Britain by
T. J. International Ltd., Padstow, Cornwall

This book is printed on acid-free paper

1

Schererzade

They said that the mother of Schererzade was a witch, and perhaps they were right: for some strange inner foresight had already told the lovely young dancer that tonight was the last time that she would ever perform at the *Ali Baba*. There was an atmosphere that she could feel above the usual haze of smoke and close, intimate laughter, a psychic foreboding that promised a climax to this particular phase of her life. It was as though the shadowy spirit of her long-dead mother had slipped across the dark lake of death and time, waiting for night when the great sun god Ammon Ra would sleep, and then creeping past Anubis, the jackal-headed god of the dead to bring a fleeting whisper of warning from the lost caverns of the underworld.

But the nightclub audience was waiting.

1

The young Egyptian officers, handsome and smiling, subdued with their wives or flaunting their mistresses; the scattering of Cairo's businessmen, and a handful of late season tourists who had strayed from the Nile Hilton Hotel; all watching and waiting. The dancer searched their faces, but at least neither of the two faces she feared most were there. There was no sign of the dark, sly face of Faizal Hassain, the Major of security police, who was her enemy, and no sign of the older, gentler face of Hamid Mehran, the army Colonel who was her lover. Even so, that feeling of finality persisted, and she determined that if this was to be her last dance then she would dance as she had never danced before.

She floated rather than walked into the spotlight, smiling in response to the sharp spate of clapping that greeted her arrival, her dark gleaming eyes promising fulfilment to the waves of expectant male faces that crowded the close-packed tables. She raised her arms, extending them in smooth brown movement like slim, rippling snakes. Her fingers touched high above her head, and there was a hush of silence as she gently swayed her hips. She stood there, smiling behind the flimsy veil that partly hid the lower half of her face. Her fine breasts were poised, the bare nipples painted with gold. The brief, one-piece costume of red silk that clothed her loins was sprinkled with golden sequins, and trailed a dozen sashes of scarlet chiffon that reached to the ground. Her brown body swayed faster as the music began behind her, and as the flat, supple muscles of her stomach stirred into controlled movement, so the slender darts of moving light radiated from the large jewel in her navel.

She danced slowly at first, her limbs moving with fluid grace. Her bare arms and shoulders followed the gently wailing notes of an Arab flute, while her hips and belly responded more rhythmically to the soft brush-beats of the muffled drums. At first her feet barely moved, her body undulating sensually in the one spot, but then as the tempo increased she began to step forward. There was no sound but for the strange Arab music, and even the breathing of the customers seemed to have stopped. Still the tempo increased, the basic spur of the drums rising above the shrill moaning of the flute. To Schererzade there was nothing else but the blind spell of music, and the driving urge to make this the supreme performance of her career. Her body whirled faster, spinning in ecstatic frenzy as she gave herself wholly to the crescendo of her dance. Some of her fervour had made telepathic communication with the musicians and they responded with an abandonment that almost matched her own. The fever-pitch of the drummer rose above all else and her mind was numb. Her body spun and shivered, writhing and bending, offering and withdrawing in a fantastic pageant of erotic expression. Her long dark hair was a flying cloud around her enraptured face, and the scarlet sashes flared from her hips. The jewel in her navel scintillated in a gyrating brilliance of movement.

The climax came in a crash of cymbals and a final, tortured wail from the upraised flute, and Schererzade ended the last dazzling spiral by falling to one knee with her arms stretched in front of her and her palms flat against floor. The echoes of the flute and the last roll of drums slowly died as she stretched her right leg full length behind her, and then the left leg full length before. The flurry of scarlet chiffon settled around her and she tossed her dark hair back on to her shoulders to look up proudly at her audience. Her gold-nippled breasts were thrust forward by her pose and still quivered with the fury of her dancing. Her whole body trembled as she smiled.

The applause broke around her like a storm of thunder, and her professional smile became flushed with genuine warmth as they expressed their appreciation. She acknowledged the shouts and cheers of some of the younger officers with brief nods of her head, and then slowly got to her feet. They demanded more, but she was still panting, and after taking her bow she stepped backwards on to the small bandstand and retreated behind the curtain. The cheering followed her as she hurried back to the cramped cubby-hole that was her dressing room, but there was to be no encore tonight.

She was relieved to find the dressing room empty, for she had half feared that either Hassain or Mehran would be waiting for her. Especially Mehran, and tonight she dreaded her lover even more than her sworn enemy, for tonight she intended to play out the last act of his betrayal.

Schererzade was a spy, and had been for the past ten years, working first for the British, and then for the Israelites. Her Arab father had died when she was five, and her mother, the old Nubian woman whom her people had called a witch, had followed him when Schererzade was fourteen. It was then that she had left the Nile village where she had been born and travelled north to Cairo. As a homeless orphan she almost starved, but her body had flowered and she was a natural dancer and ultimately she found work. At first she had danced naked in a sordid sideshow, but with age came confidence and increasing talent, and gradually she had climbed the long path that had made her one of Cairo's top dancers in the city's most expensive nightclubs.

She was seventeen when she first fell in love. She was then dancing in a small nightclub in Port Said, and the object of her affections was a young British officer who came nightly to watch her when his duties permitted. The year was 1952 and the British forces were the subject of a growing hate-campaign to speed their evacuation from the Suez Canal, and in her concern for her lover Schererzade had whispered warnings of the ugly mutterings fermenting in the city. She did not realize it was her first step into intrigue.

Soon the explosive hatred made it too dangerous for the British to stray too far outside their barbed wire encampments, and the young officer ceased to visit the nightclub. However, one night he did visit her secretly at her home, and with him he brought an older man who offered to pay her for her continued titbits of information. She knew that she was clever enough to do what they wanted, and suddenly she could sense the secret pleasure that would come from betraying the unending men who came to gloat or fondle at her young body. She had been too busy trying to survive to have any fierce sense of nationalism and so she agreed.

She did not see the young officer much more after that, and ultimately the British troops left the Canal Zone and she cried because she would never see him again. She was to have many lovers, but he was her only love.

However, she did see the older man occasionally. His name was Jackson and she soon guessed that he was an agent for British Intelligence. She did not understand why the British still wished to pay for the seemingly useless pieces of conversation that she heard in the nightclub, but she continued to supply them. An Arab who was introduced simply as Kadish acted as an intermediary and she saw less and less of Jackson.

In 1956 she returned to Cairo and a higher paid job. Later in the year Colonel Nasser, the country's new leader had nationalized the Suez Canal, causing a swift occupation of Port Said by combined British and French forces. It was a profitable period for Schererzade, for her new nightclub was much frequented by younger Egyptian officers, and reports of their comments and arguments had brought quick returns from Jackson through Kadish. She was very disappointed when the British and French forces withdrew once more.

The next few years were lean ones as far as spying was concerned, but one night Kadish came again with a new proposition. The British had no more interest in her but there were other employers. From then on her gleanings began to deflect towards Israel, and like Kadish she was happy to serve two masters. Then, a few years previously, a new intermediary appeared on the scene, an Israeli named Shabetai. She never knew what had happened to Kadish, and simply accepted the newcomer's explanation that he had retired. Shabetai was now her only contact, and the link with Jackson was broken.

It was shortly after Shabetai had appeared that she had reached the peak of her career, both as a dancer and in the gentle art of extracting secrets. She had become the star performer at the *Ali Baba*, and this once again was a night spot highly favoured by serving officers in the Egyptian forces. And for the past two years she had been the mistress of one of the top men of the Egyptian army, Colonel Hamid Mehran. Now she was approaching her greatest triumph, but by a trick of ironic fate she was also fast approaching the moment of discovery. Three nights ago she had photographed a series of top secret documents in Mehran's apartment, while the duped Colonel had laid in a drugged sleep after enjoying her favours. That film would be invaluable to Israel, but she still had to pass it on to Shabetai. She was, however, being watched by the Egyptian security police.

She did not know how or when Faizal Hassain had first started to suspect her, but she knew that he did. Hassain had started to visit the *Ali Baba* too often, watching her and saying nothing. It was possible that he came only to feast his eyes upon her body, in company with all the others, but she knew that this was not so. She sensed it. Some psychic heritage told her with absolute certainty that Hassain was a source of danger.

Hassain had guessed the truth, and only the fact that he had no conclusive proof was causing him to wait. The very fact that she was Mehran's mistress was for the moment keeping her safe, for Hassain dared not make any allegations of a brother officer's indiscretions until he was wholly sure, especially as Mehran out-ranked him.

Schererzade stood with her back to the door as the thoughts tumbled through her mind, listening to the continued cheering of the audience that demanded her return. She was sad with the thought that she would never dance for them again, and slowly pushed the door fully shut. She knew that once she had passed her film on to Shabetai then the leak would be discovered, Hassain would trace the compromised documents as

11

far as Mehran and guess the rest. She would be finished. Her only hope was that Shabetai could get her out of Egypt and that she might find safety in Israel or Europe. If it was not too late she might have destroyed the film, but now that his suspicions were aroused she knew that Hassain would stick like a leech to his task of exposing her as a spy. Her only chance was to try and get out of the country now while she had something with which to bargain — and she knew that the film could prove vital to Israel.

She dressed hastily, wincing as she plucked the jewel from her navel, and not stopping to wash the gold paint from her nipples. She put on underclothes and a dark blue dress, and around her dark hair she tied a blue silk scarf. She slipped her bare feet into a pair of sandals and then hesitated, biting her lower lip.

She was still afraid of bumping into either Hassain or Mehran as she left the club, and her nerves were suddenly keyed up to such a pitch that she knew they would sense something wrong. She knew too that she had made a mistake in performing so well, for the customers were still clamouring for more, and at any moment Moshe, the club manager, might appear and ask her to dance an extra number.

However, it was too late to change her plans now. The risks would have to be taken. She had less than an hour to make her rendezvous with Shabetai.

She retrieved the single roll of 35 millimetre film from its hiding place in her dressing table, and quickly stuffed it deep into her handbag. She went to the door, listened in case there were any approaching footsteps, and then let herself out. The shouting had died down in the clubroom now, but she could still hear the chink of glasses and the muffled laughter. She turned away from the sound and took the back way out, forcing herself to walk at normal pace and smile a calm acknowledgment to the staff as she passed through the kitchens. Mercifully she reached the staff exit without encountering Moshe.

She hurried once she was out in the street, but inside her there was a weakening sense of relief. Getting out of the *Ali Baba* was the only hurdle that she had visualized, and she felt that now she was safe. She had only to get rid of the film. The hour was late, but the streets of central Cairo were still alive beneath the flickering signs of neon Arabic, and she merged gratefully into the camouflage of the crowded pavements. Ancient buses and lurching trams still rattled past amid the flurries of spurting taxies, and the screeching, noisy tumult was soothing in its normality.

Soon she turned away into the side streets where it was darker and less crowded. The bustle faded behind her and the gutters became littered with refuse and tattered shreds of paper. The rough surface of the road harboured pools of dirty water that had been slopped around during the day by shopkeepers attempting to lay the fine dry dust. There was no traffic now, no neon signs, and only an occasional passer-by, shuffling past quickly in their long, soiled djellabahs.

She wrinkled her pretty nose against

the smells, for her features had been inherited from her Arab father more than from her Nubian mother. Her pace quickened and she clutched more tightly to her handbag, wondering why Shabetai had to choose a house in one of the dirtiest parts of Cairo for a meeting place.

She heard a car approaching behind her and moved to one side to let it pass, not troubling to look around. And then abruptly that strange sense of foreboding that had affected her before she had started her last performance in the *Ali Baba* was closing around her again, hugging her like an icy shroud in the warm night. The sharp acceleration of the car's engine roared a warning and she twisted round too late. The car was a battered American saloon that was showing no lights, and although there was plenty of room for it to pass it was coming straight towards her.

She opened her mouth to scream but the driving force of the car's nearside bumper slammed the breath from her body. Her hip bone and the darkened headlight splintered simultaneously as her slim figure was spun aside, tossed for a moment in the air before she sprawled in the gutter. The big car rushed on and vanished into the night without stopping.

Schererzade lay as if dead, her body filled with blinding pain but her mind still conscious. Again there was a moment of mental clarity, and the psychic light within her brain told her that this must be Faizal Hassain's own method of dealing with a delicate problem. Without final proof the sly-faced Major could not touch her while she still had Mehran's protection, and so he had arranged a convenient accident to remove her without any risk of recrimination.

And then, to add the final proof, a stealthy shape loomed over her as she lay helpless in the darkened road. She saw an Arab in a dark, brown-striped djellabah, his face hidden by its hood. The man smiled at her and a large, brown hand reached silently for her face. The finger and thumb closed on her nose, gently, not bruising but closing her nostrils, and

16

the palm of the hand pressed against her weakly moving mouth. She could not breathe, and she was too badly injured to put up any kind of a fight. The signs of suffocation would not show, and the verdict on her death would be a complete and fatal car accident.

2

The Gathering of the Hounds

Roger Stewart was lost. He had taken what he had hoped would be a short cut back to the Saladin Hotel, and somewhere he had taken a wrong turning that had led him into the maze of Cairo's back streets. Beside him walked his wife Veronica, his bride of six short days, her arm linked with his as she stepped daintily to avoid catching her high heels on the poor road surface. Her nostrils winced and she said cheerfully,

"Pooh! Do you always bring your wives to places that smell like this?"

Roger chuckled. "What's the matter? Afraid for your honour now that I've steered you away from the bright lights?"

She smiled. "As if I had any left!" And then she added. "But at least next time I get married I'll find a husband with a sense of direction. Admit it — you're

18

leading us round in circles."

Roger stopped and pulled a wry face, an expression that he had cultivated ever since he had discovered that it amused her. It pulled his forelock of dark hair forward over saddened eyes, and transformed his normally handsome face with an exaggerated pout of his lower lip, and he had the satisfaction of seeing her eyes brim with laughter. It was over a year ago that he had fallen in love with that laugh, and that she had fallen for what she always termed his funny face. Now, after less than a week of marriage, they had come to the joint conclusion that the delay of a twelve-month engagement had been far too long, and even while hopelessly lost in the drabbest part of Cairo they were still superbly happy.

"I concede the point," Roger said. "I haven't a clue where we are. What do you suggest, my intelligent half?"

"I'm relying on you. You're the big he-man, Doctor-Livingstone type who suggested we spend our honeymoon exploring Egypt and climbing the pyramids, et cetera; although I haven't seen the pyramids yet and I suspect that it's all a foul plot to get me away from my mother. After all, sensible people usually go to Brighton."

"You told me you had already been to Brighton," he reminded her. "You didn't like it because it had a pebbly beach."

"Stop changing the subject. How are we going to find — " She stopped suddenly. "Listen. That sounds like a car."

"So what?"

"So it might be a taxi." Veronica pulled at his arm. "Nearly all the cars in this city seem to be taxis — so few people seem to be able to afford a private car. If we're quick we might catch it and get a ride back to the hotel."

Roger saw the wisdom of her words and they hurried on again down the darkened street. The car was approaching from their left and just ahead was an intersection where it seemed most likely that it would appear. They almost broke into a run, but then the engine of the unseen car accelerated, and the roaring note told them that it was coming too fast and that they would be too late. They slowed, and in the same moment they heard a muffled crash above the thrust of the engine. The car still came on and a second later it shot across the intersection ahead and vanished in a dark blur of movement, the sound of the engine fading rapidly.

"Hell's bells," Roger commented. "He was certainly in a tearing rush to get somewhere. No lights either."

Veronica gripped his arm a little tighter.

"Roger, I think — I think he hit something."

He glanced into her face, remembering the muffled crash.

"I think you might be right. We ought to take a look."

She nodded and they quickened their pace towards the intersection. When they reached it they turned into the road to the left from which the darkened car had appeared, and saw two figures close against the wall by the side of the road ahead. One was kneeling, shapeless in a brown-striped djellabah that hung around him like an untidy nightshirt, while the second figure lay still before him, crumpled in the grip of sudden violence.

"He did hit someone," Roger exclaimed, and they hurried forward. The sound of his voice made the kneeling Arab look up sharply, and to their surprise the man suddenly scrambled to his feet and bolted.

For a split second Roger stopped and stared, but then Veronica nudged him and they turned their attention to the sprawling figure that remained. The victim was a young Arab woman in a dark blue dress, with a scarf of blue silk tied round her dark hair. Her face was twisted with pain and streaked with blood and dust where she had slithered in the gutter, and her eyes were closed.

"Roger, did you see?" Veronica's eyes were horrified and the former laughter had gone. "That man was holding his hand over her mouth. I think he was trying to suffocate her."

Roger said nothing as he examined

the still body, but after a moment he looked up.

"If he was then we disturbed him in time. She's still alive. She's badly hurt though."

Schererzade heard the words and opened her eyes. The voice and the tear-blurred vision above her struck a chord in her memory, and she recalled the young British officer of so long ago. Her breathing quickened frantically for a few seconds until she had filled her starved lungs with air, and then she said weakly.

"You — you are English?"

Roger nodded as Veronica moved to support the injured woman's head.

"Yes," he told her gently. "We're English. But don't worry now. We'll get you an ambulance and soon have you in hospital. There's sure to be somebody along in a moment."

Schererzade's mind still functioned above the pain that filled her body, and she knew that if she was taken to hospital and the incriminating film was to be found in her handbag then she would be finished. She had to get rid of it now, before the police arrived. She struggled to breathe in once more and then said,

"Listen, please. In my handbag there is a roll of film. It is very important. You must take it before the police come and — " She stopped, and realized that she could not ask these people to take the film to Shabetai, for even if they were willing they would never find him. Blackness filled her mind, and then in desperation she remembered her old-time contact with Jackson and the British. It was better than nothing and she finished feebly, "Take it to the British Embassy. They will know what to do."

Roger hesitated and she repeated,

"Please. Please, there is not much time."

Roger glanced at Veronica, and then uncertainly reached for the handbag that lay by the injured woman's side. He opened it and found the roll of film, holding it up for her to see.

Schererzade made an attempt to nod her head.

"That is it. Please go now. Before the police come. Take it to your Embassy."

Veronica said doubtfully.

"But we can't just leave you here."

"Please. You must." The dancer tilted her head anxiously as they heard approaching footsteps. "Quickly. Someone is coming. They will send for the ambulance."

Roger made up his mind abruptly and thrust the roll of film into his pocket.

"All right. We'll do as you ask. Come on Ronnie, let's go."

"But — " Veronica still hung back, but then slowly she lowered the dancer's head to the road. She stood up and Roger gripped her arm to draw her away.

"Quickly!"

The weak voice spurred them urgently and Roger tightened his grip on his wife's arm and hustled her away. They reached the intersection once more and turned the corner. Here Roger halted and waited. Less than a minute later they heard the sudden shout of alarm as a passing Arab discovered the accident victim in his path. They heard the man hammering on a nearby door to rouse some help from the occupants, and with his conscience appeased Roger turned and hurried Veronica quietly on.

After a hundred yards she said dubiously. "Did we do the right thing, Roger?"

Roger frowned. "I think so. That chap who came up behind us will probably get an ambulance on the scene as quickly as we could have done, so there was no fault in leaving her. And as for this film — I'll simply drop it into the Embassy like she said and forget about it. Whatever it is that's going on, we don't want to be involved."

Veronica nodded approval, and somewhat subdued they concentrated once more on the task of finding their way back to the Hotel Saladin.

★ ★ ★

Schererzade mercifully fainted almost as soon as the Stewarts has left, and she knew nothing of the ambulance that eventually arrived to take her to a hospital. She stayed in a coma and

26

knew nothing of the two hours she spent in the operating theatre where a team of surgeons discovered and did their best to repair a broken hip and thigh and a cracked pelvis. Afterwards she was made comfortable in a private ward, and left with a blood-drip feeding her left arm. Her name was placed on the danger list.

When she did at last recover consciousness some sixteen hours had passed, and it was almost noon. The blinds were drawn and her room was in shadow. The heat was oppressive and her body felt numbed and drained of life. She felt so terribly weak that it frightened her. Soon a watchful nurse saw that she was awake and a doctor was called. He checked her pulse and reassured her quietly, hiding his doubts behind a calm smile. He asked a few gentle questions, but she could tell him nothing of the vehicle that had knocked her down and he did not press her. Instead he advised her to rest and sleep.

She closed her eyes, but shortly after that she received a visitor. Her doctor had fended off the policeman who had wanted to question her about the accident by repeating her story that she had not been able to see any details of the car that struck her down, but he did allow Hamid Mehran into her room for a few brief moments.

The Army Colonel sat by her bedside, smiling through his anxiety. He was in uniform, but his cap was beneath his arm and she could see the iron-grey streaks in his dark hair. He was curious to know what she had been doing in the drab area where she had been found, but his concern outweighed his curiosity, for he had been warned not to tire her. She made a flimsy excuse of having left the *Ali Baba* to walk off a bad headache, and he allowed the subject to drop. He leaned forward to kiss her temple before he left, and murmured a promise to return.

Schererzade closed her eyes until he had gone, and slowly the faint dampness of tears showed beneath her lowered eyelashes. She was not in love with Hamid Mehran, but his tenderness had showed that he was in love with her, and for the first time she regretted that she had betrayed him.

She dozed, and tried to sleep. She had no conception of the passing rate of time, but abruptly she was awake again as a firm hand rested on her arm. Her startled eyelids flickered open and she stared in amazement at the man who stood over her in the gloom. She recognized the thin, intellectual face behind steel-rimmed spectacles, the high, smooth forehead and the rippling black hair that waved so perfectly that it might have been permed, and she was filled with horror at the risk he was taking, at the danger he presented for himself as well as for her.

"Shabetai!" The exclamation was sharp, even in her weakened state. "What — "

"Shh." The hiss came softly and two fingers were pressed lightly over her mouth. "You must not make a noise. The hospital staff do not know that I am here, and they must not see me."

She shivered and lay still. The Israeli was a slight, stooping man in his middle thirties, physically weak, but with a burning zeal and a sharpness of mind that could often frighten her. She liked him less than Kadish whom he had replaced, but he was a business associate and not a friend. Now he was frightening her again, but after a moment he withdrew his fingers from her lips and allowed her to speak.

"Shabetai, you must be crazy mad. What do you want?"

"You know what I want. The film you were supposed to be bringing to me. Where is it?"

Her eyes moved like nervous marbles in her head, but the only way to get rid of the Israeli was to tell him what he wanted to know. Talking was becoming more and more difficult but she managed to tell him about the English couple who had come to her assistance. His face assumed a slow expression of anguish, and at last he hissed.

"But why send them to the British Embassy? You know that film is important only to Israel."

"What else could I do?" She demanded feebly. "There is no Israeli Embassy in

Cairo. Where else could I ask them to take it?" She coughed, hurting her chest, and finished. "Perhaps the British will pass the photographs on to Israel when they have had them developed. They have no love for Egypt."

"And perhaps they will not. I do not have your blind faith in the British." He was vibrant with anger. "Describe this English couple. I must retrieve that film before they can hand it over."

"They were young. That is all I know. There was no time to ask questions." Fear and pain were beginning to take hold of her and she begged. "I cannot help you. You must go. Please go."

The Israeli stared down at her, and slowly he nodded.

Schererzade closed her eyes. She knew now that the hounds of fate were gathering at the heels of the unsuspecting couple who had helped her, but she was powerless to stop them. Instead she fainted.

3

The Running of the Foxes

Early that same morning Roger Stewart had awakened in the honeymoon suite of the Hotel Saladin. Bars of sunlight were filtering through the drawn blinds and the room was very warm. The sounds and smells from outside the window were all very different from the staid architect's office in far-off England, but for a moment his thoughts dwelled idly on the usual routine. He had a good job on the drawing board, and at twenty-eight he had excellent prospects. He also had a damned good employer who, despite the fact that he had robbed the firm of its best secretary, had cheerfully allowed him an extra long holiday in order to combine their honeymoon with a tour of Egypt. Life, he decided, was definitely rosy. The only dubious spot was the incident of the previous night, he didn't care for it much and would be glad to get rid of the film and forget the whole peculiar business.

A sleepy movement beside him sent the mixture of thoughts flying quickly away, and he returned to the subject of priority interest. Veronica nestled close against him on the wide bed, and once more he thought how lovely she looked while she slept. There were coppery lights in the long waves of her chestnut hair, and her full cheeks were flushed with a pink glow of health. He leaned forward to kiss her gently on the lips, and her long eyelashes flickered open, her large, dark hazel eyes regarding him quizzically.

"Mmmm," her mouth stirred under his second kiss. "Go easy, it's too early. Go and ravish somebody else."

He smiled. "Nobody else will let me. You're the only one on my licence."

"Ah, my gallant husband — so complimentary." She pushed him away. "Give me air. Even a wife must breathe."

Roger sat up. "Come on then, let's move. Or are you going to lay there all day, you shameless hussy?"

"You'd like that, wouldn't you? Lecherous man." She prodded him with her finger. "But I'm not. So you can just get out."

Roger pulled his funny face and saw her expression melt with laughter. He chuckled with her and then became serious.

"I suppose we'd better get up. We'll have to take a trip round to the Embassy sometime this morning. I'd like to get that job done."

Veronica stretched lazily. "You'll be lucky. Today's Sunday and the Embassy will be closed. You'll have to leave it till tomorrow."

He stared. "Is it really Sunday already?"

She nodded. "For your information we have now been married for one whole week. Three days in England, half a day in an aeroplane and three and a half days in Egypt. I might have known you'd turn out to be the sort of man who forgets anniversaries!"

Roger gave her a speculative smile. "All right, so what do celebrating honeymoon couples do on a hot Sunday in Cairo?"

"The husband takes his wife to see the pyramids," she declared firmly. "After all, if we come home from Egypt and have to admit that we haven't seen the pyramids, then people will want to know what we have been doing with all our time."

"We could always tell them the truth."

"And ruin my reputation! Not likely." She sat up and stabbed a finger at his chest. "Shame on you, sir. We are going to see the pyramids."

And so they saw the pyramids. They waited until the broiling midday heat had eased, and then walked down to Tahrir Square with its maze of green lawns opposite the great white block of the Nile Hilton Hotel. Here they caught a bus that carried them across Tahrir Bridge spanning the wide blue expanse of the Nile, and then turning south through the suburb of Giza. Like all of Cairo's public transport the bus was packed, but they accepted the sticky atmosphere and the bad-mannered pushing and shoving of the local passengers with an unshakable good humour.

After a long, eight-mile journey the unmistakable outline of the great Cheops pyramid towered ahead of them, and they left the bus to cover the last short distance on foot. After a few hundred yards the road turned right, sloping up to the three tapering mountains of stone, and a few minutes later they passed a camel stable where half a dozen of the hump-backed beasts stood or knelt in a small courtyard. A flock of Arab drivers scrambled to meet them, and they readily capitulated and allowed themselves to be mounted for the last short stage to the foot of the great burial tomb of Cheops who had been Pharaoh of Egypt forty-five centuries before.

They took photographs of each other seated on the high, swaying backs of the camels; more photographs of each other standing between the monstrous stone paws of the Sphinx; and yet more photographs against the changing background of pyramids and desert as they explored thoroughly. It was a tiring, thirsty day, but they were perfectly happy, and as it was too hot a time in the year for any noticeable amount of tourists they had the antiquities almost to themselves. They viewed the monuments from every angle, and then allowed an insistent Arab guide to show them around the maze of fourth to sixth dynasty tombs that were cut like a series of caves and tunnels into the rock and sandstone around the wide burial area.

After an exhausting afternoon they left to find a restaurant where they could get a light meal and much-needed iced drinks, but later in the evening they returned to see the *Son et Lumière*, the Festival of Sound and Light. It was a magnificent spectacle, with the massive stone head of the Sphinx and the mighty pyramids floodlit against the dark, star-pricked sky in an ever-changing pattern of red, green and golden light. The warm air was filled with stirring music, while a deep reverent voice narrated the history and the glory of the last of the seven wonders of the ancient world.

★ ★ ★

The following morning, somewhat reluctantly, they again remembered the roll of film. The excitement of the previous day had all but driven it from their minds, but the English edition of a Cairo newspaper, obligingly supplied by the hotel, helped to jog their memories. Its inside page carried a posed photograph of Schererzade in her brief dancing costume, together with a short account of the hit-and-run accident and the fact that she was now in hospital. The report added the final appeasement to their joint conscience, for they had both been slightly dubious at leaving her lying in the road, despite her insistence that they should go.

After they had both read the report Roger retrieved the film from the dressing table drawer where it had been carelessly dropped. He unscrewed the protective metal canister and took out the exposed spool. It was an ordinary 35 millimetre cartridge that would have fitted any make of camera, and there was no way of guessing what it might contain.

"I wonder what it is all about?" he

mused thoughtfully.

Veronica sat on the bed beside him and wrinkled her nose.

"I've no idea. Do you really care?"

He smiled at her. "Perhaps not. At any other time I would be intrigued, I might even be tempted to try and find out more. But right now we're on the only honeymoon holiday that we're ever likely to afford, and I don't want to be mixed up in anything else. Besides, tonight we're due to travel farther down the Nile to see the Valley Of The Kings and the temples of ancient Thebes, and that should provide us with more than enough distractions for this trip."

He pushed the spool of film back into its canister, screwed on the cap, and then dropped it into his pocket.

"Let's go," he said. "We'll drop this in at the embassy right now, and then forget all about it."

Veronica smiled wickedly and rolled back on the bed.

"Kiss me first," she instructed. "You've been neglecting your duty as a husband for at least three minutes."

When they finally left the hotel they elected to walk to the British Embassy. They had already bought a guidebook to modern Cairo and knew that it was located in Garden City, an area adjacent to Tahrir Square where most of the foreign embassies were established. They found it easily enough, crossing the Square and then following the bank of the Nile below Tahrir Bridge, but as they approached they heard the unexpected sound of a disturbance up ahead.

They exchanged wary glances, and then continued more slowly. The uproar of scuffling and shouting grew louder and more threatening as they crossed the road away from the Nile, and when they turned the corner leading to the Embassy they saw that the street was blocked by a rioting mob. Several hundred young Arabs in a mixture of local dress and European suits were massed about the Embassy gates, chanting noisily and waving placards and banners. Over a score of Egyptian policemen in white uniforms and black berets were struggling to keep the demonstration under control, screeching wildly and pushing at the mob to keep them back. Most of the policemen had short, sten-like machine pistols slung over their right shoulders, but one or two of them were using their weapons as clubs as they swiped at the more violent rioters who dodged about in search of stones to hurl into the Embassy gardens.

Veronica had stiffened nervously, and Roger's arm moved quickly around her shoulders to draw her back. He pulled her round the corner, out of sight of the mob, and then she stared up at his face.

"Roger, what — what's happening?"

"I don't know." He winced as they heard a fresh outburst of yells and the sound of breaking glass as a stone found a window, and then hazarded. "But one of those banners had Rhodesia printed in English, so I guess that must be behind it. They must be demonstrating against Rhodesia's declaration of independence. All these damned African countries seem to hold Britain responsible."

There was another crash as a second, unseen window shattered, and a fresh wave of cheering issued from the crowd. Roger risked putting his head round the corner once more and saw that the bulk of the mob had scattered into a series of running scuffles with the police. Most of the rioters were youths in their teens or twenties, and he guessed that they were students, the usual backbone of any violent protest. Some of them were spreading towards him and he pulled back. The uproar became deafening and his grip tightened on Veronica as he said grimly.

"We'd better get out of here. We obviously won't be able to get through that lot to reach the Embassy, and if they see us they might decide to get rough with us as well. Those policemen look useless, despite their fancy guns."

Veronica wisely allowed him to hurry her away. They walked fast and did not stop until they were on the other side of Tahrir Square once more and the sound of the demonstration had faded far behind them. Then they found a small bar and sat down to get their breath back and slake their dry throats with iced Coca-Cola, the universal drink. Veronica soon recovered her composure and said seriously.

"Well, what are we going to do now?"

"About the film you mean?" Roger grimaced. "I don't quite know. It'll probably take them hours to disperse that mob, so there's not much point in making another try at reaching the Embassy today, and tonight we want to be on that night train to Luxor. The whole thing's a damned nuisance."

"If we wait until the Embassy opens again tomorrow it'll mean doing the train journey in the heat of the day," Veronica said dubiously. "Either that or waiting for the night train again and wasting a whole day, and we haven't got all that much time."

Roger hesitated, and then decided abruptly. "To hell with it. We'll carry on as we planned and forget about the film until we come back to Cairo. The dust of this morning's rumpus will all have settled by then." He paused, and added. "In any case, we'll only be gone three days, and the film can't be that important."

Veronica smiled. "On this trip nothing is important — that is nothing except Mr and Mrs Stewart."

Roger inclined his head in agreement, and then to clear away the tiny feeling of doubt that still remained he solemnly pulled the wry expression that never failed to make her laugh. Her smile became broader and he kissed her impulsively, careless of the other customers around them. The film was once more relegated to a low priority.

* * *

However, despite Roger's lack of concern the unseen hounds were still gathering at their heels, and fate had already cast them for the role of running foxes. For even as they kissed a sly-faced Egyptian in a dark grey suit was making his way deliberately along one of the corridors in the large block of government departments off Tahrir Square. The man was taller than average and moved with long, silent strides. His face was exceptionally dark, even for an Arab, and his eyes were deep set with an ever-watchful glitter. Despite the plain clothes he wore at present he held the rank of Major in the security police. His name was Faizal Hassain.

He stopped before a closed door, knocked, and was admitted by a young clerk. He entered the room, one of the police administration offices, and smiled at the young police inspector writing busily behind his desk. The Inspector looked up and the resemblance between the two men was immediately apparent. The Inspector was younger, his hair perhaps a little thicker, but they came obviously from the same womb.

"Faizal!" Kamal Hassain smiled a quick greeting. "What are you doing here?"

The older brother returned the smile. "I seek a favour — a few moments of your time."

The Inspector gave him a frowning look, and then pushed aside the report he had been writing and waved a dismissal to the clerk. When they were alone he relaxed and smiled again.

"Well? How can I oblige you?"

Hassain had already seated himself, crossing his legs and making himself comfortable. He looked sideways across the desk and his quiet question had a double edge of meaning.

"Can I assume that this conversation will be in confidence?"

The younger man hesitated, and then shrugged.

"As always."

Hassain nodded with satisfaction. "Then I will explain. You will recall the street accident that occurred late on Saturday night. The one that involved the dancer from the *Ali Baba*." He waited for a nod of acknowledgment, and then continued. "No doubt you are making enquiries, but it would be counted as a personal favour if the matter were not to be pressed too closely. You understand I hope?"

The Inspector frowned. "It may be difficult, especially if the dancer dies. But as we have no clue to the vehicle that knocked her down it may be possible to have the enquiry dropped, or at least set aside."

Hassain registered more satisfaction, but there was still the most difficult question to phrase. His agent had reported the unexpected appearance of the young English couple on the scene, and in order to fully cover his tracks Hassain had to know whether or not the Englishman and his wife had realized that they had interrupted a murder attempt. He hesitated, and then asked slowly.

"The English people who found the body — is it possible to see a copy of their statement?"

He was surprised by the blank look in his brother's eyes, and by the mystified tone of his reply.

"I know nothing of any English people. According to the reports I received the dancer was found by an Arab. A shopkeeper who lived in the area."

Hassain stared at him. "But there was an Englishman, and a woman!"

The Inspector shook his head. "Not to my knowledge. But if this is true then they must have left before the shopkeeper arrived. His statement claims that he saw no one."

Hassain was thinking hard, his fingers drumming rapidly on the desk. He said aloud.

"These people rush to the scene of an accident, but before anyone else can arrive, and without calling for any help, they quickly run away again. Now why should they do that?"

"Perhaps they believed that the dancer was dead — or perhaps they did not wish to become involved with the police." Kamal Hassain was still puzzled. "But how do you — "

"This shopkeeper who found the dancer — ," The interruption was urgent. "Did his statement say whether or not she was conscious when he arrived?"

"I think she was conscious, but only for a few seconds. She could not tell him anything."

"But did she say anything to those

48

people who ran away?" Hassain gave his brother a keen, speculative look. "Kamal, I think that I must take you even farther into my confidence. That dancer was a spy. I am convinced that she was listening in to conversations between the army and air force officers who frequented the *Ali Baba*, and then reporting them to some unknown contact with Egypt's enemies. Recently so many items of information have leaked, and she is the only possible source of that leak that I can find." He paused and then went on. "Until now I had not found her presence in that strange area significant, but now I begin to wonder. She could have been meeting another spy, and if so she would have been carrying information or papers of some kind. If she passed that information, whatever it may have been, on to this young couple, then that would explain their strange behaviour in running away without reporting the accident."

The Inspector looked a little bewildered, but he nodded.

"I suppose that is a possible explanation."

"It is a possibility that I dare not miss." Hassain's fingers drummed rapidly in agitation. "I shall need your co-operation, brother Kamal. We must find this young English couple and be sure."

4

Night Train South

It was half-past ten in the evening when Roger and Veronica Stewart crossed Ramses Square, passing the great red statue of the long-dead Pharaoh and entering Cairo's main station. They had to cross to the far platform and here the scene was one of absolute pandemonium. The platform was filled with a great, writhing flood of squabbling people, all shouting and arguing amongst great mounds of huge wicker baskets and other assorted baggage. The men mostly wore long white djellabahs with scarves wrapped turban fashion around their heads, while their women were swathed and hidden in bulky robes of widow's black. Their children, in grubby pyjamas, dresses or miniature djellabahs, either wailed hysterically or sat deathly passive among the crates and boxes, many of them containing chickens or geese. The whole spectacle reminded Roger of the film that had been made from one of John Masters's excellent novels set in India.

"Ye Gods!" he said. "It's like something out of *Bhowani Junction*, only worse."

"Well, it's certainly different to Brighton." Veronica admitted. "But isn't that what we wanted?"

Roger grimaced. "Now that I've seen it I'm not so sure." Then he grinned at her. "Come on, let's see how the other half lives."

They pushed through the crush to the ticket office, and Roger joined the sprawling, disorderly queue while Veronica stood by their small suitcase and waited. The bulk of their luggage they had left at the Hotel Saladin where they intended to return, and the single suitcase carried only the necessities for their few days absence.

After ten minutes Roger returned with the tickets and found her missing. He looked around, and then caught a glimpse of the flowered dress she was wearing through the mass of jostling bodies. He pushed towards the spot and found her engaged in cheerful conversation with another young couple who were seated on heavy duty rucksacks which they had rested on the platform. She looked up as he arrived.

"Ah, here he is. Roger, this is David — and Jean. They've been telling me some blood-curdling stories about Egyptian Railways."

"They're the worst in the world," said David.

He was a big, blonde young man wearing shorts and a tartan shirt. He stood up and offered his hand, standing a good four inches above Roger who was five foot ten, and added seriously.

"Your wife's been telling me that you intend to travel third class, but I wouldn't advise it. It's like being packed into a cattle truck, except that cows would be better mannered."

Roger smiled as they shook hands. "We didn't expect luxury," he said. "We merely thought that travelling third would give a better opportunity to see the people at first hand — an experience more or less."

Jean laughed. She was an attractive girl with long fair hair, wearing a bright red blouse and white shorts.

"It will be an experience all right — but it's one that we're happy to miss. We've been staying at the Garden City Youth hostel, and most of the kids there have been down the Nile on third class trains. The stories they've told have convinced us that we'll be better off travelling first class."

David nodded. "We've been travelling cheap so far. Hitch-hiking wherever possible across Europe. We're both students from Cambridge so we haven't got too much money. Normally we've been roughing it, but for this part of the trip we're making an exception."

"We've been living soft," Roger confessed. "So it won't hurt us to try the other way for a change." He looked at Veronica and added ruefully. "In any case, I've already bought the tickets."

"And it's too late to change them." David was looking at his watch. "That train should be in at any moment."

Even as he spoke they heard the first, faint approaching rumble. The vast crowd around them began to stir excitedly and shift towards the edge of the platform. David turned to help Jean shoulder her rucksack and said quickly.

"There's another youth hostel in Luxor. If you're stopping there as well perhaps we can get together for a drink. We'll be there a few days before we move on to Aswan."

"That's an idea." Jean added emphasis to the suggestion. "The youth hostels are cheaper than hotels, and they're usually more fun. You meet some good types. Why don't you join us."

Roger smiled. "We'd like to — but there is one drawback. In a youth hostel they separate the sexes, and this holiday also happens to be our honeymoon."

"A honeymoon!" Jean looked astonished. "I would have thought Egypt was too hot for that sort of thing." Then she smiled and added warmly. "Anyway, congratulations."

"Thanks." The train was hissing into

the station now and chaos reigned again, and Roger had to shout to make his next words heard. "We can still have that drink though, we'll look you up in Luxor."

"Fine." David was swinging up his own rucksack as he spoke. "But you two had better get to the edge of the platform. If you don't make a quick dive you'll never get a seat. Jump on before it stops." The train steamed past them and as the crowds forced them apart he yelled hopefully. "We'll see you in Luxor."

Any reply that Roger might have made would have been lost in the uproar as the crowd surged forward, and for the next few moments it seemed that the whole mob had gone suddenly insane. David and Jean were lost from view and Roger had to grab hard at Veronica's arm in case he lost her also. The rush carried him forwards as the train's brakes screeched and vast clouds of steam swamped the whole confusion. The shouting and quarrelling as the horde fought and struggled to thrust their families and mountainous piles of luggage through the doors and windows was deafening, and there was a moment of near-panic as Roger thought that he and Veronica were about to fall and be trampled underfoot.

Already during their short stay in Egypt Roger had come to the conclusion that the Egyptians must be among the worst-mannered peoples in the world, and now he was convinced of it. They fought, clawed and screamed on an almost animal level, completely disregarding any but themselves in their efforts to get aboard the grossly overcrowded train. If it had been possible to turn back and travel first class on a later train he would have done so, but the clamouring mob hemmed them in behind and he could only go forward. The flood carried them through an open door, and somehow they struggled across the carriage. In the short space of seconds the seats had filled up, and baggage and people were still pouring through the windows. Roger saw an open space on one of the bare wooden seats and pushed Veronica into it, fending off an irate, rudely-shoving Arab before he could squeeze in beside her.

"Ye Gods," he said breathlessly, his words almost drowned by the bedlam. "No wonder those two students decided to travel first class. I never dreamed it could be quite as bad as this."

Veronica smiled a little wanly. "Well, we did want to see how the other half lives — remember, darling. It's the sort of experience you could never get in Brighton."

★ ★ ★

On the platform the battle still raged, and the noise continued unabated. For the bulk of Egypt's population this double railway track down the Nile valley was their only means of transport, and it seemed that the whole country must be on the move. The train was already full but still more and more people were attempting to get aboard, and amidst all this upheaval three new arrivals appeared, running hard for the ticket office. Their leader was a slight, thin-faced man who wore steel-rimmed spectacles and a dark

European suit. He thrust through the mob and rapped violently on the ticket window. The clerk began to jabber rudely, taking his time, but a handful of dirty piastre notes made him co-operate. A moment later the man was hurrying on with his two companions, and they elbowed their way through the crush to board a first class carriage with only minutes to spare.

The man in the dark suit was the Israeli Shabetai, while the men with him were both hired criminals whom he had used before. They each knew only one loyalty and that was money. Their names were Zadek and Ayoub, and for the right price they would have betrayed each other.

They relaxed as they waited for the train to move, not bothering to find seats. The two Arabs followed a pattern common in North Africa, where homosexuality is an accepted part of religion, and smiled at each other as they casually clasped hands. Shabetai ignored them, removing his spectacles and giving them a quick polish with a large handkerchief.

For the past two days the Israeli had been making widespread enquiries in search of the young English couple to whom Schererzade had entrusted the roll of film that was so vital to his country, and at last he believed he had found them. His task had been hampered by the fact that it had to be accomplished in secret, and was made doubly difficult by the lack of any proper description of his quarry, for he had been unable to revive Schererzade after she had fainted during his visit to the hospital and it had been too risky to attempt to see her again.

However, knowing that the British Embassy would be closed on a Sunday had given him a little time in which to act. He had recruited Zadek and Ayoub and started them on a systematic search of all the hotels in the area where Schererzade had been knocked down. By midnight they had drawn a blank, although there were still several hotels to check, but today's student demonstrations outside the British Embassy had been the answer to a prayer, and he was certain that the English couple would not have risked being mobbed in order to get through them. So they had been able to check the few remaining hotels. They had wasted valuable time in eliminating two likely couples who fitted the vague, youthful definition which was all that they had to work on, but finally they had enquired at the Hotel Saladin. They learned that a young Englishman and his wife were resident at the hotel, and by subtle questions also established that the couple had been out late on the night that Schererzade had met with her accident.

Shabetai had sensed that he was at last on the right track, and disregarding the glib story that had covered his earlier interest he paid the hotel's desk clerk a fat bribe to tell everything he knew about the English couple. The clerk became smoothly eager to assist, and passed on the information that the Stewarts had attempted to visit their Embassy that morning, for he had overheard them comment on the rioting when they returned. Shabetai was as convinced then as he could possibly be on such slender evidence, and decided that the Stewarts must be his quarry. He was irritated to discover that they had left to take the night train south to Luxor, and even though they were scheduled to return within three days he was reluctant to leave the film in their hands a moment longer than necessary. He had paused to make one swift phone call and then rushed to the station.

Now Shabetai finished polishing his spectacles and replaced them above his thin nose. He was still panting a little from his exertions, but the train was already beginning to roll, hissing steam above the sound of its squashed and endlessly arguing cargo, and he knew that he had only just been in time. He waited until the train had got well under way, rumbling through the dark, shabby streets of Cairo, and then clattering over the Imbaba Swing Bridge high above the black gleam of the Nile. Then he nodded to his two companions.

Zadek nodded in understanding, and somewhat reluctantly he released his friend's hand. The two separated and moved in different directions along the train, searching expertly among the passengers. Shabetai turned away and watched through the open window, enjoying the cool night breeze. He watched the tall, dark landmark of Cairo Tower moving slowly behind as the train headed south through the suburbs, and waited.

After ten minutes Zadek returned. He had investigated every first and second class carriage towards the front of the train, but all the occupants in that direction were Arabs. There were no Europeans. Shabetai merely nodded as the man finished his report, and continued to wait.

Soon Ayoub also returned, showing his teeth in a brown-stained smile. He had checked the remainder of the first and second class carriages, and had found only one couple who could possibly be English. Shabetai was pleased, for there had been no time to get an accurate description from the desk clerk at the Hotel Saladin, and so the fact that there was only one English couple simplified the task of identity. At the time it did not even occur to him that tourists who could afford to stop at hotels of the Saladin class would even consider travelling third class with the mob.

A few minutes later David and Jean both noticed the slight, bespectacled man in the dark suit who moved past and took up the seat behind them, but to them he was merely another passenger. They did look up when two white-robed Arabs occupied the seat opposite, but the dark brown faces of the two new arrivals were blank and discouraging and so they made no attempt at conversation. Instead they returned to the book of Egyptian mythology that lay open on Jean's lap, and continued their discussion on the functions of the various old-world Gods whose temples they hoped to see at Karnak. They were too wrapped up in their plans and themselves to notice anything amiss.

The train roared on into the night, gathering speed and swaying noticeably now that they had left Cairo behind.

Several times it stopped to pick up a fresh influx of passengers at smaller stations, and watching through the window they could see fresh scrambles taking place down the platform around the third class carriages. After each stop the young couple returned to their book, and they were again engrossed in their subject when the train began to slow for its fourth or fifth halt.

That was when Shabetai said softly.

"Do not be alarmed please, but this is where you are leaving the train." He smiled as their two heads twisted sharply to stare at him, and added. "Look in front of you please, and do not do anything foolish."

They looked, and saw that the two Arabs opposite were smiling slyly, and that both were holding stubby, automatic revolvers half concealed in their robes. The nose of each gun was fitted with a bulbous, screw-on attachment, and Shabetai continued.

"Those guns are silenced, and in the inevitable chorus of shouting and pushing that will arrive when the next wave of passengers come aboard I doubt if they could be heard."

David twisted angrily.

"What the hell is this? What do you want?"

"I have already told you." The train was once more hissing steam as it pulled into the station, and Shabetai was able to raise his voice without being overheard. "I want you to leave the train. You will follow me, and the young lady will come next. My two friends will follow, and should you be foolish enough to attack me they will shoot your pretty companion in the back. You will come now please." He stood up as the train gave a final jerk, and waited.

David looked from the Israeli to his two henchmen. He was angry and his first instinct was to rebel, but slowly their faces told him that they were in deadly earnest. He failed to understand, but reluctantly he got to his feet. Jean stood up beside him.

"Our rucksacks — " she began, but Shabetai cut her short.

"They are not important. Follow

closely, and remember that my friends will not hesitate to shoot."

Zadek and Ayoub had now drawn their guns back inside their robes, but although the weapons were no longer visible the threat was still there, and the folds of white cloth would do nothing to stop a bullet. There was nothing that the two young English people could do but allow themselves to be marched quietly and calmly off the train.

Once on the platform they were hustled along at a faster pace. A ticket collector came towards them, but Shabetai had thoughtfully provided himself with five correct tickets and he neatly intercepted the man while David and Jean were hurried on by the two Arabs. They were herded outside the station and across a small dusty square to a waiting car, the car for which Shabetai had hastily telephoned before boarding the train in Cairo. A moment later the Israeli rejoined them and they were forced to get into the car. David was bundled into the back seat between Zadek and Ayoub, while Jean was made to sit in the front between

Shabetai and the driver. The car roared off immediately, and was clear of the town before the Luxor train had begun to move sluggishly out of the station.

Twice David attempted to ask questions, but each time he was silenced by a curt word from Shabetai. The two Arabs were again showing their silenced automatics through the specially cut slits in their robes, and he was jabbed into fuming silence.

The drive lasted for perhaps twenty minutes, continuing south as the road followed the narrow, cultivated strip of the Nile Valley. They rushed past shadowy palms and crude, mud-walled buildings, but when the car finally stopped it turned into a grove of isolated palms where there was no sign of life whatsoever. The engine was stopped and the headlights dimmed, and the silent car stood in darkness beneath the black outline of palm fronds that partially masked the stars.

Zadek pushed open the door and got out, and a command from Shabetai made David get out behind him. Ayoub followed and the two Arabs stood close together, watching their prisoner. David glared at them, and now that he had had more time to assess the situation he wondered whether they really would dare to shoot. He dwarfed them in size, and as well as being husky and quick-tempered he had played rugger for his college. He knew that he could tackle these two skinny Arabs easily if it were not for their guns, and now that the first shock had passed he was tempted to have a go.

Behind him Shabetai had left the car and was holding Jean by the arm. The driver remained at the wheel, looking straight ahead with the blank stare of a man who wanted no part in what was to happen next.

Shabetai released Jean and pushed her towards David. The starlight gleamed very faintly on the twin black pools of his spectacles and he was smiling thinly.

"I think that you must have guessed why you are here," he said. "So if you will tell me what you have done with — "

He got no farther, for now that they were free from any possibility of interruption Zadek and Ayoub had allowed themselves to relax, and David chose that precise moment to make his move. Apart from the fact that Jean was no longer in the direct line of fire the big man had finally convinced himself that the threat of the guns must be mostly bluff. Also he had shrewdly guessed that the moment of explanation would provide him with his best chance of a surprise attack.

He was right, for Shabetai and his two lieutenants had expected him to listen to what they had to say before showing any further signs of rebellion, and all three were caught off their guard. So far Shabetai had showed no evidence that he possessed a gun, so when David dived suddenly forward in a flying tackle the target of his attack was the two Arabs. The dive was executed as perfectly as it could possibly be from a standing start, and the solid impact carried both Zadek and Ayoub crashing to the ground.

As the two Arabs yowled beneath

his crushing, fifteen-stone assault, David shouted a command for Jean to run. The blonde girl hesitated, for his move had come as unexpectedly to her as it had to his enemies, and it was Shabetai who recovered first. The Israeli lunged towards her and for a few moments she struggled wildly, clawing at his face before he managed to grip her wrists. He cursed as he pulled her around and she gave a gasping scream as he deftly twisted her arm between her shoulder blades. Holding her cruelly Shabetai reached into his pocket for the automatic that he had not previously needed.

He was too late, for in the same instant came the dull, muffled bark of another silenced gun that barely sounded above the violent battle at his feet. The tangled figures fighting in the dirt became abruptly still, shocked into silence, and then slowly they rolled apart. Zadek lay to one side, bleeding from a hefty punch in the mouth, his head shaking dazedly. A yard away crouched Ayoub, breathing harshly and still levelling his gun. Before them David's large body sprawled motionless and there was a black stain on the breast of his tartan shirt as his wide open eyes stared up at the night sky that was just visible through the close palm fronds.

Shabetai swore savagely, for within another few seconds he would have knocked the Englishman unconscious with his own gun. He blistered the two hapless Arabs with his tongue, but finally he calmed and became more rational. He ordered Zadek to hold the girl, and stood between her and the body as he said grimly.

"Mrs Stewart, I am sorry that this has happened. Your husband acted foolishly and my men were equally stupid. But I still want to know what happened to that roll of film that was given to you on Saturday night."

Jean was staring past him. David's death had numbed her mind and she was feeling sick and dizzy inside. Only the first two words had registered, and when she looked up she said weakly.

"My name isn't Stewart. It's Peters — Jean Peters. And David wasn't my husband. We were not married." The words broke her restraint and she began to cry.

Shabetai opened his mouth, stopped helplessly, and for the first time he realized that he had blundered. He wheeled on Ayoub in a fit of fresh anger, cursing and ordering the man to search the dead body. The Arab found the final proof in a body belt that was strapped around the dead man's waist, a British passport that identified their victim as a student named David Marsh.

There was a long silence, and then in Arabic Ayoub asked for further orders. Shabetai hesitated, and then gave them in a bitter voice. He turned his back on the scene and moved away, gazing up grimly to where the stars twinkled through a gap between the palms. He was glad that the girl did not scream, and when the echoes of the second shot had faded away into the thick shadows he turned wearily to supervise the double burial.

5

Luxor

Throughout the long jolting night Roger and Veronica were able to doze only for brief moments, and were rudely awakened at every station. The train was so fully packed that it was impossible to move the doors which opened inwards, and so the windows provided the only means of entry and exit for the swarming passengers and their baggage. At each stop there was a fresh outbreak of squabbles and argument, and the Stewarts had to endure steady streams of Arabs of all ages and sexes climbing over their laps. They finally gave up trying to sleep altogether, but avoided deep despair solely by concentrating their joint sense of humour on the funniest side of the whole glorious confusion. They had wanted some unusual experience, and they had to admit ruefully that they had most certainly got it.

When dawn at last brightened the sky they were still awake, and despite being tired and hungry, and filthy with the dust that had blown in through the open carriage windows, they were still able to smile. The crush had mercifully thinned out somewhat when the train had stopped at Asyut, and the rest of the trip became less of an ordeal.

In fact, now that it was daylight they began to enjoy the strange new scenery of the Nile Valley. There were fascinating Nubian-style villages, the crude dwellings made of plastered mud and dried dull brown by the sun, and around them green, irrigated fields of maize or cane and endless tall, slanting palms. Often the Nile itself was visible, its broad, placid surface speckled with drifting dhows, and often too there were glimpses of the arid desert beyond the pitifully narrow strip of the fertile river valley.

The journey lasted until noon, and by then they were not only tired and hungry but streaming sweat in the fierce heat. They were heartily relieved when the train at last steamed into the station at Luxor, and despite the inevitable stampede they managed to climb out of the nearest window on to the platform. The direct sun grilled them as Roger helped his wife down and they stood weakly by their single suitcase. Veronica automatically raised a hand to shield her eyes.

"The glare," she winced painfully. "Roger, we really must get some sunglasses and some big floppy hats. Otherwise I'm sure we'll both get sunstroke."

He nodded. "We'll make that a priority move. We really should have got them before we left Cairo. It wouldn't be a bad idea if we took the example of those two students at the same time and got ourselves some shorts. At the moment my jeans are practically glued to my legs."

Veronica agreed, and then squinted around the platform.

"Speaking of David and Jean — where are they? They said they'd see us at Luxor."

Roger twisted his head to look both ways along the platform, and then said.

"They've probably got away already.

There wouldn't have been such a crush to hamper them around the first class carriages, and in this heat they must have decided not to hang about." He bent to pick up their suitcase, and then took her arm as he finished. "We'd best get moving too, before we're roasted alive. We can look them up later at that youth hostel they mentioned."

Veronica was feeling too deflated to argue, and so they followed the main mass of disembarking Arabs and found their way out of the station. In the dusty square outside they found two or three pony-drawn traps for hire, and allowed the nearest one to convey them directly to the Winter Palace Hotel where they had already reserved a room. They checked in at the desk and went immediately upstairs where they stripped off and shared a shower for ten delicious, laughing minutes. And then they lay on the wide double bed, pulled a single thin sheet over their bare bodies to protect them from mosquitos, and thankfully caught up on their lost sleep.

★ ★ ★

They awoke when the worst heat of the day was over, shared another cold shower, made love almost automatically, and finally dressed and descended to a light meal. It was then evening and after satisfying their hunger they went out on a shopping expedition to better equip themselves for the sweltering climate. On the way back they remembered the two students from Cairo once more, and after enquiring the way from a shopkeeper who had just sold them iced drinks, they sought out the local youth hostel.

It was an easy place to find, being less than a hundred yards up a side street that was directly opposite the great columns of Luxor's imposing temple. They went inside and found a young Arab boy behind the counter. The youth spoke good English, but he merely shrugged when they mentioned David and Jean. He told them that at that moment he had no English people staying at the hostel. Germans yes; and a party of Frenchmen; even a Swiss — but no English. And in any case there were no girls, at present, the girls' dormitory was empty.

Roger was puzzled, and explained that his two friends should have arrived on the noon train from Cairo.

The youth shrugged again. No one had arrived at the hostel from the noon train. No one at all. Then, as though sensing that his word was in doubt, he offered them a small pile of Y.H.A. identity cards and invited them to check for themselves.

Roger hesitated, but realized that he would only cause offence if he accepted the offer, for David and Jean were obviously not here. Instead he thanked the youth, and then he and Veronica returned outside.

"It's strange," Veronica said. "I wonder what could have happened to them?"

Like the youth in the hostel Roger could only shrug.

"Perhaps they stayed on the train," he suggested. "They mentioned something about visiting Aswan, so they may have decided to do that first. I suppose they were interested in the new High Dam that the Egyptians are building."

"Perhaps," Veronica echoed dubiously. "But I'm positive that David spoke as though they were stopping here first."

"Well perhaps they stopped somewhere else. At Asyut for instance. Everything got so garbled in the rush to get on that train that we probably misunderstood what they did say."

Veronica nodded, but she was still frowning. Roger took her arm and began to lead her away.

"Let's go and explore that temple," he said. "We'll look in here again tomorrow, and probably find that they've turned up with some perfectly logical explanation."

★ ★ ★

Later that same evening Schererzade received a visitor in her private ward at the hospital in Cairo. She was off the danger list now, and apart from the general lethargy that followed shock and a dangerous loss of blood she was in relatively little pain. The whole of her body below the waist was still stiff and immovable, and she dreaded to think of what lasting damage might have been done to it. But at least her mind was clear and for long periods she was conscious. She was lying in darkness when her nurse appeared to switch on the light and admit her visitor, and there was a panicky moment of guilt as she thought that it must be Mehran, but her guilt turned to a keen shaft of fear as she saw that it was not her Army lover who stood in the doorway. Her visitor was Faizal Hassain.

The tall Major came towards her bed, smiling politely as the nurse left the room and closed the door behind her. Hassain was bareheaded and again wore dark civilian clothes. He sat on the chair by the bedside, and behind his smile his deep-set eyes held a faintly malicious gleam. Quietly he asked her how she was feeling.

Schererzade knew that this man had tried to have her secretly killed, and despite her thumping heart she felt a quiver of revulsion as she attempted to smile and answer his outwardly friendly question. Hassain nodded as though pleased, and it was then that the dancer's fear began to show as she asked hesitantly.

"Why have you come to see me?"

"Why should I not come to see you? A dancer has many admirers, and I am merely one of the many who has enjoyed watching while you entertain." The smile reappeared on his dark face, and he added obliquely. "Perhaps you can entertain me again."

Schererzade tried to keep her voice steady, but her nerves were still jittery as she said slowly.

"How can I do that?"

Hassain continued to smile, and his hand moved to lightly caress her shoulder through the thin silk of the hospital nightdress. She shivered from his touch and tried to draw her body deeper beneath the bedclothes, and then he answered softly.

"Do you remember the stories of the *One Thousand And One Nights*, and the beautiful princess whose name you adopted as your own, even though you have slightly changed the spelling? That Schererzade saved her own life night after night, by telling stories to entertain her Sultan who would otherwise have chopped off her head." He stroked her cheek with his finger and finished. "I thought that perhaps you might care to save your life — by telling stories to entertain me."

Schererzade lay still, not daring to draw her face away from the icy touch of his hand. She knew that he must be very sure of himself to challenge her so openly, but she struggled to keep her head. She said feebly.

"I am sorry. I don't — I don't understand you."

"Then let me explain." The smooth voice was as soft as ever. "Today I have questioned more closely the Arab shopkeeper who found you lying in the street after your accident, and he has proved to be a surprisingly observant man. He saw a man and a woman run away and leave you as he approached, and what is more he is ready to swear that the man took something from your handbag before he left and that you urged him to depart. When he made his first statement to the police he did not consider these facts worth mentioning, but he has been quite prepared to adjust that statement after more detailed questioning."

Hassain paused there, and again he stroked her cheek.

"Let us be frank," he said at last. "I have long suspected that you were a spy, and now that this new evidence has told me where to find the proof I have only to apprehend this man and woman who came to your assistance and you are finished. Whatever it was that you managed to pass on I shall find, and the very fact that you acted so desperately to avoid having this mysterious something found on your person tells me that it must have been wholly incriminating." His sly smile returned and he added. "But you can still make my task easier by telling me exactly what it was that you passed on to these people — whether it was papers, film, a tape recording, or whatever it might have been. That is the story which you can tell that might save your life. That and the identity of these people and whatever instructions you gave them."

Schererzade looked away and said dully.

"I am sorry. I still do not understand you."

A harsh hand gripped her jaw, twisting her face back again, and now Hassain's eyes were glittering like those of a baulked wolf.

"You are a fool," he told her. "I happen to know that those people were English, and as you should know all English and other foreigners are obliged to register as aliens with the police department within three days of their arrival. I already have men checking that aliens file, and as there are very few tourists in Egypt during midsummer it will not be difficult for me to track down the particular two that I want. It is only a matter of time."

He pushed her head away and stood up, towering over her.

"You could have made things simpler for me, and I gave you your chance.

You refused it and now you can face the consequences for your spying." He glared at her and fired his final shot. "When your friends are caught not even your Army lover will be able to save you. In fact, I doubt if Colonel Mehran will be able to save himself."

6

At the Temples of Karnak

On the Wednesday, their first full day in Luxor, Roger and Veronica were roused at half past four in the morning in order to explore some of the area's splendid monuments before the sun could reach its full, murderous height. The modern town of Luxor was built upon the same soil as Homer's hundred-gated Thebes, and had been the home of Egypt's mighty Pharaohs fifteen hundred years before the birth of Christ. Across the far bank of the Nile lay the great barrier of ochre-yellow cliffs that guarded the funerary temples of Ramses and the great Queen Hatshepsut, and behind them lay the almost legendary Valley of the Kings where lay the royal tombs of the Pharaohs, including the tomb of Tutankh-amun. While at the south end of the cliff barrier lay the Valley of the Queens, and the tomb of

Nefertiti, the most beautiful of all the Queens of ancient Egypt.

However, for their first day the Stewarts had decided to stay on the East bank of the Nile, for here, less than half an hour's walk from their hotel, were the great ruined temples of Karnak. Dedicated to the Gods of Sun and Moon, the basis of early Egyptian religion, the colossal ruins ranked among the oldest and most magnificent that remained on earth.

They declined to stop for breakfast, but accepted instead a picnic basket which they carried with them, and it was nearing five o'clock as they set off to walk along the bank of the Nile. The way was shaded by graceful palms, and in the stillness of early morning the pale grey waters lay like some broad dream river into fantasy, unrippled by a single dhow. It was a pleasant stroll, comparatively cool, and they were in just the right mood to enjoy themselves.

It was a short walk, and it seemed that all too soon they had reached Karnak. They approached past an avenue of stone rams, many of them still intact, and entered the great temple to the Sun God Amun Raa. The entrance was guarded by massive stone pylons, and they felt positively dwarfed as they passed through the gap between the twin barriers. The left hand pylon had crumbled to almost half its original height, but its opposite number still towered to its full one hundred and forty feet.

They explored slowly around the great inner forecourt, wandering through the adjoining temple rooms and regarding everything with awe. There were no other tourists, and apart from the Arab watchman drowsing near the entrance they had the place to themselves. Soon they found a flight of steps that enabled them to climb to the top of the broken pylon, and from here they had a wide, sweeping view of the whole fascinating maze of ruins. Beyond, beneath bright green splashes of palms, lay the mud walls of the village dwellings, and to the west across the placid Nile lay the distant wall of desert cliffs.

The sun was strong now, and they were already glad of the headgear they had purchased the previous evening. Roger wore a straw panama hat, while Veronica had chosen a wide-brimmed, mexican-styled sombrero. Roger was also wearing his new shorts, but Veronica, wary of having her knees and thighs burned by the sun, had decided to wear another light cotton dress. They donned their sunglasses as the glare was again becoming painful, but as the view was so compelling they elected to stay on top of the pylon and make their first attack upon the picnic basket.

Roger sat with his legs crossed in eastern fashion and gazed down at the courtyard and its broken columns below them.

"Can you just imagine a modern construction firm attempting to build something that would last as many hundreds of years as these have done," he said seriously. "And doing it without the aid of derricks and bulldozers and rattling great concrete mixers. They just wouldn't know where to begin. Those old-time architects must have had a stupendous imagination to conceive all this, knowing that they had only bare hands with which to build it."

Veronica nodded casual agreement from behind a chicken sandwich, but her mind was more romantic than practical and she dismissed the problems of construction as she remarked.

"Can you picture it as it must have been in the past? In all its splendour when it was clean and white, and filled with colour and masses and masses of people. Perhaps there were handsome princes with gleaming swords, and nobles and ladies in all their gold and finery; merchants and warriors, and fast chariots rushing through that very courtyard. The Pharaohs themselves once walked there, and swarms of big black slaves. Lovely princesses and — "

"And more handsome princes," he finished for her.

She laughed. "Yes, lots and lots of handsome princes. And I'll bet they didn't go around showing their knobbly knees off either."

"Then you'd lose," he said cheerfully. "In those days the men wore dinky little leather skirts, and they had the knobbliest knees you ever saw. They also had a nasty habit of having their wives chopped up and buried with them when they died, so you can count yourself lucky that you're married to a fine civilized Englishman, rather than some fancy Egyptian prince. Mind you," he added, "the princesses were all right. They were all dark-eyed beauties, celestial virgins skilled in the arts of love."

"How could they be both?" demanded Veronica, switching abruptly from the romantic back to the practical.

Roger grinned. "I think they all read Doctor Kinsey. They knew the theory anyhow."

They continued their happy banter, munching through sandwiches and drinking plastic cups of iced lemonade from the large vacuum flask that had been packed in the hamper, until abruptly they realized that there was nothing left. They had intended to save some for later, but Roger merely shrugged and commented that now they could leave the basket with the watchman at the entrance instead of having to carry it everywhere with them. By then it was becoming uncomfortably hot, and so they left their lofty perch and descended to the courtyard.

The Arab watchman readily agreed to mind the basket until they returned and they continued their explorations. They passed into a vast hall of one hundred and thirty-four huge columns, some still topped by massive stone lintel blocks, that towered seventy feet above them. Each monstrous column was painstakingly carved with the outlines of Gods and Kings and a whole treasury of hieroglyphic signs. Veronica had already learned some of their meaning, and knew that the asp and the sun symbolized power, while the scarab and the key were symbols of luck and life. With this limited knowledge, and the often repeated pictures of the Gods and sacred animals, she attempted to piece together the wealth of history and myth that was written in stone. Her camera clicked like the tune of a busy typewriter, while Roger was equally happy selecting shots to record the design and construction rather than the decoration. They were unlikely to ever return, and so they were both shamelessly extravagant with their film.

It was shadowy and cool beneath the monolithic columns, and when they finally moved into the full sunlight again they found that the heat was now really fierce. However, there was still much to see and they moved on into the connecting temple where the lofty obelisk erected by the long-dead Queen Hatshepsut soared like some incredible carved needle into the searing blue sky.

The ruins became less definable now, and they wandered among fallen walls, great blocks of masonry, broken columns and chipped statues. They turned to their right and found the sacred lake that had once served the temple priests, but now it was more like a stagnant, half-filled swimming pool.

The great temple to the Sun God was behind them now, but ahead lay the ruins of four more impressive pylons, and over to their left the temple of the Moon God Khonsu, the son of the Goddess Earth and Amun Raa. The third of the four pylons was undergoing some form of reconstruction and was surrounded by a hotch-potch of crazy wooden scaffolding and a swarm of Arab workers, and so the Stewarts chose to make for the far corner and the temple to the Moon God.

This temple was smaller than the sprawling mass of ruins devoted to Amun Raa, but it was almost intact with many of the heavy roof slabs still in position and was an equally imposing monument. They passed between the guardian pylons and found it to be full of dark, cavernous chambers that made a cool haven of refuge from the merciless sun. They heaved sighs of relief and sat down upon a block of stone to change the films in their cameras.

"Phew, isn't it hot," Veronica murmured. "No wonder we have the place to ourselves. We've really picked the wrong time of year."

Roger smiled, and flexed his shoulders to free his sweat-soaked shirt from his back. "You should have married me before," he said. "Then we could have come out in April. It's your own fault for playing hard to get."

"It's you who should have tried harder," she contradicted. "You might not have appreciated me if I had surrendered too easily." She took off her sombrero and shook loose her waves of chestnut hair. "But anyway, I'm still melting."

"Me too." Roger handed back her camera and finished. "We'll explore this place, and then call it a day. The sun is right overhead now, and we've still got to walk back to Luxor."

She nodded and replaced her hat, and they rose once more to continue their explorations. Everywhere they had been the columns and walls had been smothered with carvings and inscriptions and the walls here were no exception. Veronica recognized the hawk-headed figure of the Moon God, and then Osiris the Judge of the Underworld together with Anubis the jackal-headed God of the Dead, and once more she forgot the heat in the excitement of her discoveries. She lingered to adjust the aperture and shutter speed of her camera, while Roger meandered on with his head tilted back to wonder how the great slabs had originally been raised to cover the roof.

His interest sharpened when he found a flight of steps leading upwards, and he turned to give Veronica a shout. He saw that she was still engrossed with her wall carvings and then changed his mind, deciding to ascertain first whether the steps really did lead on to the roof or whether they merely stopped in a dead end. He was in luck, for a moment later he came out into blinding sunlight again, standing on the temple roof with a fine view of the ruined scene around him. He lifted his camera and for the moment Veronica was forgotten.

In the temple below she had finally dragged herself away from the carvings, and although she could no longer see him she assumed that he was ahead. She wandered on idly, still gazing curiously into every nook and corner, but the sight of some fresh carvings distracted her away from the half concealed flight of steps. There was a peaceful hush beneath the dark columns and walls, and she was quite content to walk alone. A blaze of sunshine and the promise of more light for her photographs drew her into a square chamber where there was no roof, and as she passed through the narrow doorway a hand closed firmly over her mouth.

It was so utterly unexpected that she could neither yelp nor struggle. Her camera dropped, bouncing on her middle as it was suspended by the strap round her neck, and in the same moment her arm was twisted behind her and she was dragged swiftly backwards into the corner of the room. Her eyes went wide with terror and she twisted her head violently, seeing a brief glimpse of the man who held her. He had a thin, intellectual face with a smooth forehead, black crinkly hair that was so perfectly waved that it might have been permed, and wore a pair of steel-rimmed glasses. Then another twist at her arm made her be still and she could do nothing but watch. On either side of the door through which she had just entered stood a silent Arab. They were both armed with strange, fat-muzzled automatics, and they waited absolutely motionless for Roger to amble in behind her.

For a whole minute the bizarre tableau remained in frozen stillness, but contrary to all their expectations Roger failed to appear. The two Arabs looked uncertain, and flashed puzzled glances towards their leader.

Shabetai was also at a loss. It seemed that he had encountered nothing but frustration and delay during the past few days, and he was wary of making any more rash mistakes. He had blundered badly on the train, but fortunately he had known from the desk clerk at the Hotel Saladin that the Stewarts would be staying at the Winter Palace Hotel here in Luxor, and despite an infuriating breakdown that had cost him half a day on the road it had been simple enough to find them once he had completed the journey down the Nile Valley. He had learned that the Stewarts were at present visiting Karnak, and deciding that here would be as good a place as any to deal with them he had followed. He had arrived just in time to see them entering the temple to the Moon God, and so he had slipped in through a side door with his two companions to lie in wait. Now it seemed that ill luck was once again playing havoc with his plans, and only one of his intended victims had walked into his ambush.

He hesitated, but this time he wanted to be positive that he had caught up with the right couple before taking any further action, and so he twisted the frightened face of the girl towards him, knocking off her wide sombrero hat in the proces. He said softly.

"I assume that this time I am speaking to Mrs Stewart. Nod your head please if I am correct."

Veronica stared up at him. Her flustered mind was searching desperately for some way of warning Roger, but for the moment she was helpless and could only move her head slightly forward as instructed.

Shabetai pursed his lips grimly, and then looked towards the waiting Arabs.

"The man must be somewhere in the temple," he said in a low voice. "You must find him and bring him back here."

As he spoke he was holding Veronica's head hard against his chest, his left hand still clamped rigidly over her mouth. He released her arm with his right hand and reached inside his jacket pocket to produce his own silenced automatic. He held it under her nose to warn her to remain still, and then nodded his head to start Zadek and Ayoub on their search. As they left he moved Veronica nearer to the doorway so that he could surprise Roger if the two Arabs should miss him and he came searching for his wife.

On the roof above Roger was still scrambling happily over the great stone slabs that made up the irregular levels, pausing every few moments to aim his camera. Having reached the roof he had assumed that Veronica was sure to find the flight of steps and guess where he had gone, and so he had followed the tempting urge to climb as high as possible before he turned back. Then he saw the square opening in the roof and went towards it, wondering whether he would see Veronica below. He moved quietly, hoping to surprise her, but it was he who received the first surprise.

He stared for one long, unbelieving moment, and slowly his handsome face stiffened with anger. Roger Stewart had a friendly and amiable outlook upon life, and up to a moment ago he had not possessed a care in the world. But the unexpected sight of a strange man cruelly manhandling his helpless wife was like a red rag to a healthy young bull.

His first impulse had been to shout, but he bit the exclamation down as he saw the gun. He didn't know what was going on but without hesitation he moved to stop it, circling silently around the opening and taking care that his shadow did not fall inside. Directly above them he knelt, and once again peered down into the temple. The man with the gun was obviously awaiting his own arrival, but Roger had no intention of walking into the trap. Instead he gripped the edge of the roof and swung his body inside. He released his hold the instant his full weight jerked upon his arms, and regardless of the fearful drop that could easily have broken both his legs and his neck, he plummeted straight down on to Shabetai's shoulders.

The Israeli heard the sudden movement and his face twisted upwards in alarm. For a split second he saw the hurtling body dropping out of the sky, and then his startled yell was cut short as Roger's feet thudded into his right shoulder and slammed him violently to the ground. Both Roger and Veronica crashed down on top of him and for a moment they were inextricably mixed.

Fortunately for Roger the Israeli's body had broken his fall, but even so the effects were almost as paralysing to him as they were to the luckless man underneath. They both lay gasping in agony and it was Veronica who struggled up first and had the presence of mind to secure the fallen gun. She turned to help Roger and he had to lean against her heavily, wincing with pain as a trickle of blood ran down his knee from an ugly bruise. Shabetai was still helpless, groaning wretchedly.

Quickly Veronica explained that they had two more enemies searching the temple, and although he still had not quite grasped what was going on Roger allowed her to hustle him out of the sunlit chamber. He was limping badly and still breathless, but at least he had no broken bones. They started back through the first of two columned inner courtyards, and then abruptly Zadek and Ayoub appeared ahead.

Both parties stopped. The two Arabs had already received one lashing reprimand for shooting too hastily, and this time they were briefly hesitant of opening fire on their own initiative. On the other hand, the irate Roger was still obsessed with the need to protect his bride, and grabbing Shabetai's automatic from her hand he fired an angry shot that ricocheted among the columns and sent both Arabs diving frantically for cover.

He pulled Veronica back behind the corner of a wall, and for a moment he was undecided as to his next move. The two Arabs were between him and the main entrance, and although he guessed that there must be side doors to the temple he could easily trap himself in a dead end if he attempted to search blindly. Then he realized that he was again within a few yards of the flight of steps that had tempted him on to the roof, and so he chose the route he knew and retreated upwards.

Below him he could hear the two Arabs moving closer, and he fired another blind shot to teach them a little respect. The silenced automatic made only a muffled spitting sound, but the whining of the bullet as it pinged waspishly from column to walls was frightening enough, and neither Zadek or Ayoub were inclined to rush the narrow stairway. Roger's knee was throbbing hideously, and he considered it a miracle that he had not smashed the knee-cap, but with Veronica's help he reached the roof and emerged for the second time into the dazzling sunlight.

The two Arabs still hesitated inside the temple, reluctant to make any definite moves. Then Shabetai reappeared again, stumbling clumsily towards them. The Israeli was still wheezing badly and clutching weakly at the right shoulder that had taken the whole terrible force of Roger's two-footed arrival, and his thin face was practically bloodless with pain. His glasses were askew and he almost fell as he said furiously.

"Get after them, you fools. And remember that I want them alive."

His hirelings still held back, and savagely Shabetai wrenched Zadek's gun from his hand. He knew that the two Arabs would only follow if he led the way, and rallying his battered body he plunged up the narrow flight of steps in pursuit of the two fugitives.

7

Gunfire at Karnak

By the time Shabetai appeared on the
temple roof Roger and Veronica had
already scrambled across to its lowest
level. Here there was another long,
desperate drop to the ground, but
this time there was soft sand below
and despite his misgivings after his
first reckless descent on to Shabetai's
shoulders Roger nodded to Veronica to
go ahead. She wriggled over the edge,
hung at arm's length for a moment,
and then allowed herself to fall. She
landed well, rolling forward on impact
and then climbing quickly, if shakily,
to her feet. Roger turned to see their
pursuers heading towards him, and then
followed her down.

He landed more clumsily, and sprawled
in the sand with a fresh wave of throbbing
spreading from his bruised knee. Veronica

helped him to his feet, and again he was limping badly as they set off at a lurching run back towards the vast ruined temple of Amon Raa. Behind them Shabetai and the two Arabs reached the edge of the roof, and Ayoub was already raising his gun.

"Shoot low," Shabetai hissed. "Aim for their legs."

The suppressed bark of the automatic was barely audible, but Roger saw the spurt of sand suddenly fly up a yard to his left. He turned, levelled his own gun, and saw them all throw themselves flat as he jerked the trigger. He carried on running then with Veronica by his side, and when he next risked a quick look back he saw that his three enemies were dropping to the ground and again taking up the chase.

Roger's first instinct had been to head for the main exit from the enclosed area of the monuments, but as they ran towards the temple of the Sun God he realized that the three men behind would probably anticipate such a move, and so he veered more to the right. He found an entrance that led them through to the great hall with its mammoth columns, and turned directly away from the forecourt and the giant pylons that marked the entrance.

Another bullet smacked near his feet and he twisted round to catch a glimpse of Ayoub dodging back out of sight through a gap between the columns. His limp had enabled the three men to close the gap between them and desperately he used his gun again to keep them at bay. He jerked the trigger twice, and the first time a bullet bounced wildly through the columns. The second time the gun jammed.

Roger swore, and then continued his flight, still with his left arm locked around Veronica's shoulders. He zigzagged through the titanic colonnades and came out into the wide central roadway close to the majestic Hatshepsut obelisk. He had no intenton of crossing that open stretch, and like a hunted fox he doubled once more to his right.

By now they were almost spent, and were streaming sweat as they fought for breath. Above them the high sun blazed with impartial ferocity, and now that they had both lost their protective hats they were beginning to feel weak and dizzy. Roger's limp had worsened to a painful hobble, and now that the gun was useless their plight was almost hopeless. They stumbled on through fallen columns and walls, and then abruptly they found a gap that brought them out facing the sacred lake once more.

Their route had now brought them roughly along two sides of a square, and they could again see the temple to the Moon God in the far corner of the enclosed area. Nearer to them however, was the line of four ruined pylons which they had previously ignored, and around the third monument in the line the squad of Arab workmen still busied themselves like large, slow-moving ants. For all Roger knew Egypt might have suddenly declared war upon Britain and he might be running into still more trouble, but it would not be many minutes before the men behind him realized that he was unable to return their fire any more and so he had to decide quickly. He pulled at Veronica and they began to run again towards the workmen.

They were in the open now and hurried as fast as they could possibly go, expecting at any moment that more bullets would start flying behind them. They circled the sacred lake and reached the ruins of the first pylon, and only then did they dare glance round. They saw Zadek appear, and then duck back hastily to call his armed companions, and they added an extra spurt to their pace.

To their utmost relief no further shots were fired, and as they passed the second pylon Roger realized that their pursuers dared not continue shooting now that they were in sight of the working party. Consequently, they slowed their pace to a casual walk, and Roger pushed the jammed automatic into the pocket of his shorts out of sight. So far, despite all the violent activity, there had been no shouting, and as all three of the automatics had been fitted with silencers the working party were unaware that anything abnormal had been taking place.

Roger needed time to think and for the moment he preferred the situation to remain that way.

They stopped close to the third pylon and stood watching, as though taking an interest in the reconstruction work that was going on. It was hard to tell what was actually being done, as the crumbled remnants were almost hidden beneath the rickety patchwork of wooden scaffolding, but there were nearly a score of Arabs engaged on the task. The fugitives sucked in long breaths of the hot, dry air, and attempted to steady the racing beat of their hearts. Then Veronica glanced over her shoulder.

"Roger, they've stopped. What are we going to do?"

He looked back and saw that the three men had halted by the sacred lake and were looking momentarily baffled.

"I'm not sure," he admitted. "What the hell did they want anyway?"

"I honestly don't know. They just grabbed me, and then two of them went to look for you. Then the next thing I knew you were dropping out of the sky." She looked up at him with sudden anguish. "Roger, you shouldn't have done that. It was crazy — You might have killed yourself."

He pulled a woebegone face and reached down to rub a careful hand against his furiously aching knee.

"I can see that now," he said. "But at the time I didn't stop to think."

They glanced back again and saw that Shabetai and the two Arabs had moved a little closer, and instinctively they began to circle behind the hive of activity that surrounded the pylon. Roger knew that he could probably enlist the aid of the gang of workmen if he was to explain to them what had happened, but that would ultimately mean that the police would be called in and he was strangely reluctant for that to happen. He didn't quite know why he was wary of being involved with the Egyptian police, although his subconscious reasons were to become apparent later, and so he was undecided as to what they should do next. For the moment they had a reprieve, but they could not stand here for ever, and now that Roger could barely hobble it was impossible to renew their flight.

Their presence had now been noticed, and several of the workmen were making grinning comments, posing themselves on the hotch-potch of scaffolding and indicating that the tourists should use their cameras. Roger had almost forgotten that his camera still dangled on his chest, and he made a pretence of smiling and clicked the shutter a couple of times in an effort to look natural. At the same time he was racking his brains and trying to keep one eye open for any further moves from their enemies. Their gradual retreat took them behind the pylon and there they had a stroke of luck. Veronica suddenly nudged his elbow, and Roger saw a dust-stained Jeep standing only a few yards away.

Beside the Jeep stood a man in dark trousers and a white shirt and tie, issuing a stream of instructions to two of the Arab workers in their djellabahs. The collar-and-tie man held a clipboard in his hand, and he finally detached some papers, presumably drawings, and gave them to one of the Arabs before nodding dismissal and turning back to his Jeep. Roger guessed that the man would be heading back to Luxor, and hurried swiftly forward to beg a ride.

The man's dark face became immediately doubtful. The Jeep, he explained in hesitant English, was government property, and he was an official of the Department of Antiquities responsible for the monuments. Much as he would like to help them he was not officially allowed to do so. He pointed out that in any case Luxor was only a short walk, and that if they wanted to ride they should have arranged for a taxi.

For a moment it seemed that Roger must fail, and that the fussy official's refusal was final, but then he tried a new approach on a more tactful line.

"I do understand," he said. "But unfortunately my wife has been taken ill. We are not accustomed to such terrible heat, and the sun has made her sick and dizzy. A few moments ago she fainted, so perhaps in the circumstances — ?"

The official looked dubiously at

Veronica. After the gruelling experience she had just been through she was still flushed and sweating, and really did look as though she had only just recovered from a spell of fainting. The man hesitated for a few seconds, and then his attitude became helpful.

"I apologize," he said. "If the lady is not well then this is a different matter. Of course, you must ride with me to Luxor." He took her arm tentatively to lead her to the Jeep, and his teeth flashed in a solicitous smile.

Roger heaved a sigh of relief, but their escape was not yet accomplished. The white-collar man's change of attitude was a complete reversal, and now he insisted upon dithering to arrange a cushion for the *sick lady* to ensure her comfort. Roger could only wait anxiously and pray that their three enemies did not realize what was happening in time to interfere.

At last Veronica was seated in the front of the Jeep, and Roger thanked their rescuer as he climbed into the back. The official grinned cheerfully, and then suddenly remembered some last minute instructions that he had forgotten to impart, and delayed for another agonizing minute while he called over one of the working party. Then at last he climbed into the driving seat and started the engine. The Jeep bumped erratically as he slammed it into gear, and the wheels threw up clouds of dust as he roared over to the far side of the enclosure. For the first time Roger realized that there was a gate here, and that it was not necessary to go back towards the main temples where they would have to pass the three men who had attacked them. A watchman wearing an untidy turban and a dirty grey djellabah opened the gate as they approached, and their driver gave the man a cheery wave as the Jeep rattled through. A moment later they were on the road back to Luxor.

Roger relaxed, feeling that he could now admit to absolute deflation from the overpowering heat. They were now on a parallel road to the one which they had followed along the Nile bank that morning, and were speeding through tall palm groves that shaded the mud-brown dwellings that formed the village of Karnak. To their left their driver pointed out another, smaller enclosure that contained more, lesser temples built around a second sacred lake, but Roger found it difficult to show even a polite interest.

They passed camel and donkey riders, and soon they were driving back through the dusty streets of Luxor. Veronica was looking pale and unsteady, and now that their driver had committed himself he gave her a steady stream of reassuring smiles and finally dropped them right in front of their hotel. Roger thanked him profusely, and then he turned the Jeep round and vanished down the Nile road with a brisk wave of his hand.

Still feeling immensely relieved Roger helped his wife into the hotel, and as quickly as possible they hurried up to their room. They collapsed wearily upon the double bed and lay side by side, breathing heavily as they regained some of their energies. The strength-sapping heat had left them feeling like limp rags, but in the comparative coolness of the hotel they slowly began to recover.

At last Roger was obliged to move, due to the painful pressure of Shabetai's gun jabbing into his groin as he lay face down. He rolled over and sat up, tugging the offending weapon from the pocket of his shorts. Veronica stirred slowly, and stared into the bulbous nose of the automatic.

"Roger," she ventured in a low voice. "Why *did* those men attack us? There must have been some reason."

He remained silent, thinking, but finally he said.

"I can only see one possible answer — and that is that it must have been something to do with that damned roll of film that we should have taken to the British Embassy in Cairo. We read in the newspaper that the dancer from the car accident was still alive, so presumably she must have passed on the fact that she was able to give the film to us. Whoever she told now wants to get it back. That's the only way that I can reason it out."

"But they tried to kill us!"

"No," he contradicted. "All their shots were fired low, so I think that they must have been trying to hit us in the legs, or else frighten us into giving up. Either way they wanted us alive."

He laid the automatic on the pillow and then moved closer to her, putting his arm around her shoulders as they sat together on the edge of the bed.

"Try and think," he urged. "Did they say anything when they grabbed you? Anything at all."

Veronica wrinkled her brows.

"There was something. The man who was actually holding me, the one who wore glasses, he said, '*I assume that this time I am speaking to Mrs Stewart*,' or something like that, and told me to nod my head if that was correct. I couldn't speak because he kept his hand over my mouth."

Roger frowned, and began to repeat, "*I assume that this time* — " He stopped there, and the truth began to dawn upon them both in the same moment as they stared into one another's eyes.

"Roger, you don't think — "

She couldn't finish, but Roger nodded slowly.

"It definitely implies that they've made a previous mistake. And if they did mix us up with another couple then it explains why David and Jean haven't appeared here in Luxor."

"But how could they have got us muddled up," Veronica argued. "David was so big and blonde, while you're smaller and dark. And Jean was blonde too, whereas my hair is dark brown. It doesn't make sense."

"It does if they didn't know what we looked like. They had to ask you if you were Mrs Stewart, so it sounds as though thy tracked us down somehow but only managed to get our names plus the fact that we were heading down here to Luxor."

"But how?"

He shrugged. "Darling, I don't know. Perhaps we'll never know. But we must face the facts. Three men attacked us this morning, almost certainly because of the film. And it also seems almost certain that they were responsible for the disappearance of David and Jean. They must have assumed that we would be travelling first class, and our student friends must have been the only English couple on that part of the train. That must be how the mix-up was made. The point is, what are we going to do about it?"

Veronica was doubtful.

"Go to the police?" she suggested uncertainly.

Roger shook his head. "I don't think so, not in this country. The Egyptians have no real love for the British, even though they're keen enough to take the tourists' money. They still smart over Suez and they hate us in Aden. If we went to the Egyptian Police and told them the truth then they would realize that we originally intended to take the film to the British Embassy, and would probably arrest us as spies." He was realizing now that this subconscious knowledge was what had kept him from being frank with the workmen at Karnak, and he finished slowly. "We'll only be in more trouble if we go to the police. Our best plan is to take the next train back to Cairo, retrieve that film from the luggage we left at the Hotel Saladin, and then go straight to the British Embassy. Once we give them the facts they will be able to do more than we can towards helping David and Jean."

Veronica was still unhappy over the fate of the two students, but finally she agreed that Roger's plan was best. He kissed her gently as a form of reassurance, and then moved to the bedside telephone to call up the manager of the hotel. He enquired about the train service to Cairo, and made up the excuse that the midsummer heat was proving too much for them and had decided them to cut short their stay. He listened to the manager's regrets and then turned back to Veronica.

"There's a train at six o'clock this evening, so we'll be taking that. Meantime, we'll have a shower and then get packed, and I'll see if I can un-jam that gun so that we can be on our guard."

He reached for the automatic, but Veronica stopped him.

"First things first," she said. "Come

into the bathroom and let me bathe that knee. It looks terrible."

"Roger hesitated, and then obeyed, and they were still in the bathroom when a sharp knock sounded upon the outer door a few minutes later. They exchanged glances, and then Veronica fastened the last safety pin in the bandage she had just affixed before they returned to the main bedroom. Roger eyed the door warily, and then he decided that their enemies would hardly dare to approach them in the hotel and crossed the room to open it.

The man who faced him wore a white uniform, and there were two policemen in the corridor behind him. He smiled calmly and said.

"Mr Stewart? I am Inspector Kamal Hassain of the Cairo police, and I believe that you can help me with some of my enquiries."

8

Return to Cairo

Roger stared dumbly into the Police Inspector's face. The man was about his own height, with the same medium heavy build, but he was older, in his late thirties, and his dark face had the look of accustomed authority. His eyes were deeply set above the large Arab nose, and his mouth was a little too thin to allow his smile to be wholly pleasant. He had not troubled to remove his peaked cap, and without waiting for Roger to answer he pushed his way gently into the room. The two policemen blocked the door behind him and stood motionless. Their white uniforms looked baggy and grubby compared to the crisp smartness of the Inspector, and they wore black berets, and machine pistols slung over their right shoulders.

Roger found his voice and said sharply.

"What enquiries? What's this all about?"

Kamal Hassain nodded politely to Veronica, who now stood uncertainly beside the bed, and then he turned to answer.

"I am enquiring into a street accident that occurred in Cairo late on last Saturday night. I understand, Mr Stewart, that you and your wife were the first witnesses on the scene, yet you ran off without reporting the accident to the police. Can you explain why you should do that please?"

Roger's mind grappled desperately with this new turn of events, but all that he could immediately think about was the silenced automatic that lay in full incriminating view on the pillow of the bed only a few yards away. He didn't dare look towards it, and with an effort he held the Inspector's gaze as he answered.

"There's no mystery about it. We just didn't want to be involved as witnesses. There were other people arriving to help the injured woman, and as we didn't actually see the accident, or the car that was responsible, there was no additional way in which we could have helped." He forced a smile and explained. "We're not only on holiday, Inspector. This is also our honeymoon, and we didn't want to spoil it."

Hassain looked towards Veronica and asked smoothly.

"Do you agree with that statement, Mrs Stewart?"

Veronica nodded her head. "Of course, that's exactly what happened."

Roger tensed for the exclamation as the Inspector saw the gun on the pillow, but Hassain merely inclined his head in a formal gesture, and then turned to speak in Arabic to the two policemen. Baffled, Roger looked for the gun, and saw that it was not there. The pillow had been disturbed, however, and he realized that Veronica had been sharp enough to push the gun out of sight. He relaxed, but immediately his nerves tightened up again as the two Egyptian policemen moved past him with the obvious intentions of searching the room. He started angrily to protest, but Hassain simply repeated his bland smile.

"I am sorry, Mr Stewart. But I am afraid that I cannot fully accept your explanation. You see, the young woman whom you found after that street accident was a known criminal, and the fact that you approached her and then ran away again without offering any practical assistance strikes me as very suspicious. Especially as another witness has made a sworn statement to the effect that the dancer passed to you some small object or written message before you hurried away from the scene. It is that unknown object for which my men are searching now, although it would help if you were to tell me exactly what it is."

"This is ridiculous," Roger snapped. "All that we did was to fail to report a street accident. And you're trying to make that look like a major crime. It's utter nonsense."

"Failure to report an accident is an offence," Hassain retorted coolly. "And in view of the circumstances I feel obliged to investigate more fully."

Roger fumed inwardly, but he could see no advantage in antagonizing the man with any further protests, and so he moved to stand by his wife and watched. The two policemen were thorough, examining all the dressing table drawers and searching through all their belongings, but as they had not brought the roll of film to Luxor Roger became slowly confident that the search would draw a blank.

Then one of the policemen, a fat-faced little man with a bristly moustache motioned him to stand aside, and he realized with dismay that the man intended to turn over the bedclothes. He moved reluctantly, and a moment later the policeman gave an excited shout as he discovered the gun beneath the pillow.

Kamal Hassain made a mock show of raising his eyebrows as he reached out to take the automatic. Then he looked at Roger and murmured gently.

"A dangerous-looking weapon, and fitted with a silencing attachment. Do you have a permit for this, Mr Stewart."

"No," Roger said shortly. "It isn't mine."

"I see. Perhaps you can explain then how it came to be in your possession. You must realize that carrying a firearm without a permit is yet another, and far more serious offence against the law."

Roger looked at Veronica, but her lovely, dark hazel eyes were empty of any advice. She was even more at a loss than he was, and it seemed that now the police were actually on the point of arresting them they could lose nothing more by telling the truth. He turned back to face the Inspector and launched into the full story of the incident at Karnak. At the same time he reasoned that a full disclosure of the facts might save some delay in finding David and Jean, and so he added his strong belief that the men who had attacked them at the temples were responsible for the disappearance of the two students.

Kamal Hassain listened intently, but he had no interest in the two missing students. He waited for Roger to finish, and then said pointedly.

"But why did these three unknown men attack you at Karnak? Were they also trying to recover that mysterious something that was passed to you by the injured woman in Cairo?"

"There was no mysterious something," Roger retorted bluntly, for he was not yet ready to admit that part of the story. He realized that in theory the only real crime that they might have committed lay in retaining the film instead of handing it directly to the police, but he was not pleading guilty to that charge until he had received some definite legal advice from a representative of the British Embassy. Unless the police found the film they could not prove the charge anyway, and so Roger continued to bluff. He said forcefully.

"Perhaps those men believed that we were carrying something that they wanted, but they made a mistake. Exactly as you have made a mistake. I don't understand why you should both believe that we accepted some object or message from that poor woman, but it's all some kind of confused misunderstanding. I have no more idea of what you might be looking for than you have."

The statement was uttered boldly, and should have been convincing, but Hassain showed no sign of apology. When he spoke his voice was as smooth as before, and again he was faintly smiling.

"Let us assume that I believe you. You are innocent, and you have nothing to hide. Yet at Karnak you were violently assaulted by three perfect strangers who chased you through the temples firing bullets at your feet, and you have made no attempt to complain to the police here in Luxor. How do you explain this strange fact? You also speak of two English students, who you say have vanished. Surely this is another incident that should have been reported. Why have you not done so?"

Roger said wearily. "We haven't time. We have only just returned from Karnak. You arrived before we could even telephone to the local police station."

"I understand," Hassain said politely. "If I had not arrived you would have made your report to the police here in Luxor. Then what?"

Roger looked at him blankly. "What do you mean?"

"I mean what would you have done next? You would have waited, I suppose, to see that these would-be assassins were apprehended. And then you would have continued your holiday like normal tourists. Tomorrow you would have crossed to the west bank of the Nile to visit the remaining temples that you have not yet seen, and of course the fabulous tombs of the Pharaohs that are Luxor's greatest attraction. After all, as innocent tourists it is these wonders that you have come to see. Am I not correct?"

Roger saw the gaping trap, and remained stubbornly silent.

Kamal Hassain nodded with slow satisfaction. "You do not answer," he observed. "Because you have guessed that I have already spoken to the manager of this hotel. You did have time to telephone before I arrived, but you had no intentions of calling the Luxor police. Instead you enquired about the time of the next train back to Cairo. That was not the action of an innocent tourist, Mr Stewart. That was the action of a man preparing to take flight, a man who must have good reason to avoid both his attackers and the police."

His voice became sharper and he finished grimly. "I think that you should return to Cairo, both of you. But you need not wait all afternoon for the next train — you can return with me in a police car."

* * *

The journey back to Cairo took them twelve hours, and Kamal Hassain was clearly in a hurry. Roger and Veronica were given enough time to pack their one suitcase, and then under a police guard they checked out of the hotel and entered a large black saloon that waited outside. They were allowed to sit together, squashed in the back with the fat little policeman with the moustache, while the second policeman took the wheel and the Inspector relaxed in the front beside him. The car was already

134

a literal oven of heat, but they set off immediately.

It was a gruelling drive, for they were travelling through the hottest part of the day and the temperature was somewhere around one hundred and twenty degrees fahrenheit. The car's windows were kept open, but the dusty air that rushed inside was like a blast from a furnace door and did nothing to cool them. Neither of them felt like talking in the presence of the three Egyptians, and so they sat in dull silence.

The road, like the railway, paralleled the Nile, never straying from the narrow green valley that held the life blood of Egypt. They bumped through mud villages and small towns, beneath the never-ending necklace of feathery green palms. In the fields the peasants toiled by hand, or with primitive bullock-drawn ploughs. Naked children swam and played in the muddy irrigation channels, and groups of women clustered with their big, earthenware pots around the wells. There were great, golden mounds of corn, being threshed by tireless bullocks pulling heavy sledges in endless circles to crush the grains, and everywhere the scenes were sprinkled with camels, goats and donkeys. Frequent views of the Nile, and of the great barren desert waiting beyond the narrow valley added to the fascination of interest, but the Stewarts were in no mood to enjoy it.

Hassain stopped twice on the way to Asyut, giving them brief respites from the cramped car. Each time they entered a cheap bar in one of the small towns, and the Inspector politely offered his two prisoners refreshment. He was smoothly courteous, and it seemed that he was quite content to leave any further questioning until they arrived at Cairo.

At the second stop there was a change of drivers, and the fat policeman with the moustache took the wheel. He drove them into Asyut, the chief city of Upper Egypt, and as this marked the approximate half way mark of their four hundred mile journey they stopped for a longer break at a police station. Roger and Veronica were given a meal, but after six hours of travelling through the awful afternoon heat they both felt too exhausted even to eat. The only privilege they appreciated was the chance to wash some of the dust and sweat from their arms and faces.

After an hour they took to the road again, but mercifully the sun was setting and soon it was night. The policeman who shared their back seat began to doze in his corner, and Veronica rested her head upon Roger's shoulder until she too slept. Roger was also feeling desperately tired, but he endeavoured to stay awake so that he could more carefully support her.

They made one more stop for a final change of drivers, and then sped continuously through the night until they finally reached Cairo in the early hours of the next morning. Roger roused himself as they entered the lighted streets of the city, and realized that he had been sleeping for the past few hours. Veronica was still fast asleep beside him.

He roused her gently as the car halted outside the police department building, and wearily they allowed themselves to be taken inside. The Inspector walked ahead of them and led the way to his office. He nodded to them to be seated, and went behind the desk to use the telephone.

The calls he made were in Arabic, so Roger had no idea of what was being said. The fat policeman was now standing by the door behind them, and Roger could only sit in silence and wait. He glanced at Veronica and saw that her face was pale and strained. He reached for her hand and squeezed it gently, giving her a reassuring smile as she looked towards him. He felt sure that so far the police did not have sufficient grounds to hold them for any length of time, and although he had received no chance to tell her so he was relieved to see her smile faintly in return.

Kamal Hassain finished his telephone calls and sat back in his chair. He idly contemplated on the ceiling until Roger broke the irritating silence to ask.

"What was all that about?"

The Inspector eyed him carelessly. "Just a few routine instructions. I have ordered one of my sergeants to take your suitcase over to the Saladin Hotel. He will take another man with him, and while they are there they will search through the rest of your luggage for — " He shrugged. "For whatever it is that we are looking for."

Roger's confidence underwent a sudden shaking, for he had not expected that a second search would be made through the baggage that they had left here in Cairo. After the first search had failed in Luxor he had hoped that the Inspector would eventually admit defeat, and assume that even though his suspicions might be correct he was too late to prove them. Now he realized that Kamal Hassain did not admit defeat so easily, and if Schererzade's roll of film was found in their hotel room after they had denied its existence, then he and Veronica would be really in trouble. He hesitated, and then said.

"I think this has gone far enough. I demand to see someone from the British Embassy."

Hassain smiled. "That will be allowed, I assure you. But at the moment it is an awkward hour in which to disturb them, and there is someone else who wishes to meet you first."

Roger's irritation showed, for he was fast beginning to loathe that smooth smile. Then Veronica touched his arm and shook her head in quiet warning, and he forced himself to relax. She was right and there was no point in losing his temper.

They sat in silent exasperation for the next five minutes, while the Inspector calmly studied some reports on his desk. Then there was a knock on the door, and all three looked round as the attending policeman quickly held it open.

The man who entered was taller than Kamal Hassain, his face was thinner and so was his dark hair. He was older and his dark suit clashed with the Inspector's white uniform, but despite these differences the family resemblance was still strong. There was the same thin mouth and the same deeply-set eyes. The two smiled fondly at each other, and then the Inspector said formally.

"This is the man who wishes to question you further. He is a Major in the police department responsible for the security of the United Arab Republic."

9

Flies in the Web

The sly-faced Major was silent for a moment, carefully concealing his deep, inner satisfaction. He stood like some tall, calculating stoat, assessing the most likely method of ensnaring two nervous rabbits. His dark face was expressionless, yet he carried with him his own black aura of secret power that marked him as by far the most formidable enemy that they had yet encountered. Roger's anxiety increased, for he sensed instinctively that with this man against them then he and Veronica were fast approaching really deep water. The Major studied them both, and then looked up and said quietly.

"Thank you, Kamal. You have been very efficient. But now I think that I would prefer to talk to these young people alone." He paused delicately. "I

142

would also be happier if you were to take personal charge of the search at the Hotel Saladin."

The young Inspector nodded briefly. "I will leave immediately, and ensure that nothing is missed. Meanwhile you may have the full use of this office, and my man will wait outside the door to ensure that you are not disturbed."

The arrangements suited the tall Major, for his teeth showed in a fleeting smile. Kamal Hassain adjusted his cap and started to leave, and the taller man followed him out into the corridor. They closed the door and Roger could hear the faint mutter of their voices as they talked for a few moments in low tones. Then the Major returned alone, and the policeman by the door moved outside as he had been ordered.

Roger watched as the man in the dark, sombre suit moved past him to sit down, facing him from behind the wide desk, and he felt that events were sweeping forward much too fast for him to stay upon his feet. The appearance of the Egyptian security officer had made him fully realize that he was involved in something dangerous and big, but for the moment he could see no better course of action than to sit tight and hope for the best. It was too late to expect any leniency by admitting everything at this stage, so he could only pray that the film would not be found.

On this last point he suffered an even finer agony of mind, for he did not even know where the film was hidden. Veronica had handled it last while they were packing for their trip to Luxor, and so far he had received no chance to ask her what she had actually done with it.

The Major relaxed with his elbows on the desk, and with the tips of his fingers placed together to form a careful pyramid in front of him. It was a stance he found useful when he wished to intimidate his subject, for with his hands partially concealing his own face he could emphasize the deep-set glitter of his eyes. He said quietly.

"Perhaps I should introduce myself. I am Major Faizal Hassain, and as my brother, the Inspector, has told you my task is to ensure the security of the United Arab Republic. Now, perhaps you may not appreciate this, but you may be endangering that security." He paused, and then continued in the same tone. "I think that if I decide to be more frank with you, then you may feel inclined to reply in the same spirit. The Inspector told you that the woman who was knocked down in the street accident you witnessed was a criminal, but this was not exactly so. She was worse. She was a nightclub dancer who performed under the stage name of Schererzade, and we have strong reasons to believe that she was a traitor and a spy. So you understand that if you did perform some small favour to oblige this woman, then you too can be charged with espionage. If this is the case, then the only course that can benefit your own position is for you to be wholly truthful to me now."

He had been watching Roger, but now his eyes strayed to Veronica, rested a moment, and then moved back. He lowered his prayer-like hands and placed

145

them flat upon the table, and then he smiled.

"Now that you understand — have you anything that you wish to tell me?"

Roger was sorely tempted to take the inviting little speech at its face value, except for one small thing — he didn't trust the Major. His first impression had been that here was a man with a cold and devious mind, and that impression was growing stronger with every moment. He knew instinctively that Faizal Hassain would suffer no conscience from lies and false promises, and again his impulse was to refrain from any admission of guilt. He said flatly.

"I only want one thing. And that is to be allowed to speak to someone from the British Embassy."

"But why, Mr Stewart? If you are innocent of having helped this spy then you will be released with our sincere apologies as soon as possible. It is only if you are guilty that you will need the legal advice which is all that an embassy official will be able to give you."

The Major leaned back in his chair as

he delivered this piece of logic, and again he made a pyramid of his fingers, hiding all but the glitter of his eyes.

"I will ask you again," he said softly. "Did you, or did you not, accept some object or written message from the injured woman before you left the scene of the accident?"

Roger faltered for a minute paring of a second. But the lie had already been told and could not be worsened by repetition. He said bluntly.

"No."

Faizal Hassain looked steadily at Veronica.

"Perhaps you would care to be more reasonable? Or do you agree with your husband?"

Veronica moved nervously in her chair, but she did not make the mistake of looking to Roger for guidance. Neither did Roger have to look at her, for he knew that whether she agreed with his handling of the situation or not she would never fail to support him fully against any outsider. She met the Major's direct gaze and said briefly.

"Of course I agree with my husband!"

"How very loyal," Hassain remarked. "But hardly wise." He looked back to Roger and continued. "In view of your repeated denials I feel that I must be even more frank. The police at Luxor have failed to find any trace of the three men who attacked you at Karnak, nor of the two students whom you claim have vanished. Now this does not mean that I do not believe your story, for on these points I am inclined to believe you implicitly. In fact I am practically certain that those three men at Karnak must have been Israeli agents. The Israelies are Egypt's sworn enemies, and it is on their behalf that the dancer has been conducting her spying activities."

He leaned forward again, resting his elbows once more on the table. "Now what I want to impress upon you is this. The men who attacked you are the allies of the woman whom I think you may be trying to protect. So you must see that you owe her nothing. In fact, if your silence enables her friends to remain free, then their freedom may once more prove dangerous to you if I am obliged to release you through lack of evidence."

Again it was an impressive speech, and Roger had to admit that the Egyptian's logic was making sense. But still he hung back. There was yet a chance, even though a slim one, that the younger Hassain would fail to find Schererzade's roll of film, and while that chance existed he was determined to sit tight.

The Major was silent, waiting for a reply, and gradually his dark Arab face became harder. A hint of sharp exasperation played around his mouth, and his fingers began to drum slowly along the edge of the desk. Then abruptly the telephone rang.

He picked it up and listened, twisting around in his chair so that neither Roger nor Veronica could watch any change of expression that might have registered on his face. The muffled voice from the telephone, together with his own replies, were all in Arabic. Roger's heart was pattering swiftly as he listened, for he was sure that the caller must be the

Police Inspector reporting on his search of their hotel, but even so he took the opportunity of exchanging glances with Veronica and gently squeezing her hand. Her fingers responded quickly to his own, and inwardly he blessed her for the way in which she was bearing up under the strain. Then he had to release her as Faizal Hassain lowered the telephone, and swung thoughtfully back to face them.

The Major rested the phone on its cradle, and again his fingers drummed on the edge of the desk. Then he reached a decision, stopped his drumming, looked up and smiled.

"It seems that I owe you an apology," he said. "The Inspector has just reported the results of his search, and it seems that there is nothing among your baggage that might have been passed on to you by the dancer. For the moment, therefore, I must assume that the witness who saw you leave the scene of Saturday night's accident made either a false or exaggerated statement."

Hassain had risen slowly to his feet as

he spoke, and momentarily Roger could only stare at him, only half believing their good fortune.

"Does this mean that we are free to go?" he demanded.

The Major nodded and moved around the big desk.

"For the moment, yes. But I must retain your passports and warn you both that you must not leave Cairo until I have completed more enquiries. There is still the question of the men who attacked you at Karnak, and when they are apprehended you will be required to identify them."

Roger got to his feet and Veronica pressed beside him. He put his arm around her and said hesitantly.

"We'll be glad to identify them, if you can catch them."

"Thank you." Faizal Hassain inclined his head politely. "And in the meantime I hope that you will accept my apologies, and a car to drive you back to your hotel. This misunderstanding must have caused you a great deal of worry, and you are obviously tired."

Unexpectedly the Major offered a lean brown hand, and Roger gripped it hesitantly. Hassain's grip was cold and strong, but Roger was ashamed to find that his own hand was trembling slightly with relief. The Major made the same gesture to Veronica, and then called to the policeman outside the door to escort them down through the building.

* * *

Ten minutes later they were deposited on the pavement outside the Hotel Saladin by the same police car that had brought them up from Luxor. Its driver bade them a courteous goodnight and then continued almost immediately on his way, and for a few minutes they simply stood and breathed the free night air of Cairo. They had kept up their long silence while in the car, and still without talking they made their way inside the hotel. Roger collected their key from the sleepy but curious desk clerk and they climbed wearily up the stairs to their room. Roger closed the bedroom door behind them without bothering to switch on the light, and only then did Veronica relax and cling limply in his arms.

"Oh, Roger," she sobbed weakly. "That was horrible. I was so sure that they were going to throw us into some smelly Egyptian jail. I can hardly believe that we're free."

He leaned his shoulders against the wall and held her trembling body against him, stroking her face and nuzzling his cheek against the dark softness of her hair. He too was feeling greatly relieved, but he was more controlled.

"Ronnie darling, take it easy. You've been wonderful all day and now it's all over. They didn't find anything so we're in the clear." He switched on the light and smiled at her, seeing the wet stains in her dark hazel eyes. "It's all over," he repeated. And then he sought her mouth and kissed her fiercely.

She clung to him with desperate passion, as though she had feared that they might never embrace again. Her mouth was as hungry as his own, and it was several minutes before they parted.

She seemed to have drawn from some of his strength and her body was less tense, her eyes were still damp but now she could smile.

"That's a woman's privilege," she said wryly. "Going all tearful and weepy. Like having babies and being underneath in bed, and all the other things we're entitled to. You'll just have to get used to it."

He shrugged grandly. "I think I can bear it. I have a very manly and absorbent chest. It soaks up tears like nobody's business."

Their playful intimacy was evident for a moment, but then relief intruded once more and he took her back into his arms. They kissed impulsively for the second time, and then they moved into the centre of the room as he said seriously.

"I think we're safe now, but I must admit that I was far from being happy at the time. That oily Major was one of the most distasteful types I've ever met, and I am sure that his toady brother couldn't fail to find that film. I kept quiet because it seemed to be the only possible chance we had, but I never really expected that we would get away with it. Like you, I can hardly believe that they have really let us go."

They stood for a moment, looking around the room. The drawers and wardrobes were all closed and the place looked neat and tidy, and it was hard to believe that it had been searched at all. Roger assumed that this was because the searchers had been careful, and had not been restricted by time, but he failed to understand how they had missed the object of their task. He turned to Veronica, holding her shoulders, and said helplessly.

"Ronnie, tell me something — what exactly did you do with that blasted film? Where did you hide it?"

She made a bewildered face. "But, Roger, I didn't hide it anywhere. I just put it with all the others and left it in the bottom drawer of the dressing table."

He blinked. "What others?"

"Why, our films of course. The films we used around the Sphinx and the Pyramids, and at the Citadel and all round Cairo during the first two days we were here. Between us we exposed about six rolls, so I put them altogether."

As she spoke she pulled open the bottom drawer of the dressing table and lifted out a flat cardboard box. She took off the lid and revealed seven small tin canisters of exposed film that lay beneath a sheaf of notes. Six of the seven canisters had been numbered with a felt pen, and Roger recognized the notes they had made for their own guidance when they came to sort the eventual photographs into sequence, for they had noted down details of time and place and focusing figures for each shot.

"Well I'll be damned," he said. "When they searched here they must have glanced at our notes and saw that these were obviously tourist films we'd taken ourselves. They missed the fact that there was one unnumbered film with no relevant notes." He held up the canister in question and smiled broadly. "What a stroke of luck that it was ordinary 35 millimetre like the rest — and damned smart of you to mix them up."

"I wasn't trying to be smart," Veronica confessed. "It was just that all the instruction sheets stress that film should be kept in a cool dry place. So I thought they would be out of the heat."

Roger grinned. "I don't care why you did it. You fooled the opposition and saved us from spending the rest of our time in Egypt in a prison." He bowed forward and kissed her neatly on the nose as he finished. "Did anyone ever tell you that you're a marvellous wife?"

"Only a few," she said modestly. "Just some of the princes and millionaires I turned down in order to marry you." She sat down upon the bed and then became serious again. "But we're not quite out of the wood yet, Roger — we've still got to get rid of that film. And we haven't got our passports."

Roger sat beside her. "We'll sort that out in the morning," he assured her. "Or perhaps I should say later today. We can't possibly be unlucky enough to run into a student riot twice running, so we'll pop the film straight into the British Embassy. Once we've done that we've disposed of the evidence, and we can leave it to the Embassy to get our passports back from the Egyptians. Then we'll go home."

Veronica looked dubious. "I'm not so sure, Roger. I think we ought to destroy that film now, and forget that we ever saw it. I have the feeling that that Egyptian Major only allowed us to go because he wanted us to lead him to the film, and if we try and take it to the Embassy tomorrow that will be just what he expects. He'll be waiting for us like some horrible, fat spider in its web."

Roger stared at her, and suddenly he knew the truth.

Veronica went on seriously. "They didn't miss the film because I happened to mix it up with our own. They missed it only because they didn't really know what they were looking for. But that Major knew we were guilty, Roger. Letting us go was simply his way of giving us enough rope to hang ourselves, and if we try to take the film to the Embassy then that's exactly what we'll be — "

She broke off abruptly. "Roger, what's wrong?"

Roger was already standing up, and moving slowly towards the bathroom. He said bitterly.

"Ronnie, I have a sinking feeling that we have already hung ourselves. Like dutiful little flies we've already walked into the Major's web."

He reached for the bathroom door, knowing that he should have made this simple check before they had started talking, and certainly before they had committed themselves by retrieving the film. He pulled the door open and his sharply aroused suspicion became proven fact.

For smiling at him calmly was the bland face of Kamal Hassain.

10

Flight by Dhow

The young Police Inspector stepped almost mincingly into the bedroom, looking highly pleased with himself. He removed his peaked cap and made a little bow towards Veronica, and then he smiled once more into Roger's face.

"How very unfortunate," he said smoothly, "that your good wife should help you to realize the danger only when it is too late. As she has so rightly guessed, we had to let you lead us to the object of our search, for it was pointless for us to continue searching blindly. Now, however. I think it should be possible to have the traitorous Schererzade transferred from her hospital bed to a jail, where you can both join her in a long prison sentence for spying."

Roger was utterly disgusted with the way in which he had been so casually tricked, for now that everything was clear it seemed impossible that he had not had the forethought to realize what was happening. Right from the start he had sensed and distrusted the devious mind of Faizal Hassain, but even so he had failed to see behind the Major's slick change of tactics. He had to accept the bitter fact that he was a mere amateur against these calculating experts, and that they had quite nonchalantly showed him up for a fool.

The expression on his face must have revealed his savage feelings, for Kamal Hassain said warningly.

"Please do not make any further tedious mistakes, for I have two policemen waiting in the corridor outside. You have lied your way into your present position, and if your honeymoon ends in separate cells then that is entirely your own fault. Now will you please pass that roll of film to me, and then we will all return to Police Headquarters and the Major."

He held out his hand complacently for the film, but he never received it. The smug use of the word *tedious* had been enough to turn Roger's bitterness into rising anger, for it implied that he was nothing more than a minor irritation and rubbed sorely at his pride. But the reference to separate cells and the accompanying look of anguish that had appeared upon Veronica's face had touched an even deeper nerve, and killed any possibility that he might have submitted tamely. As with Shabetai before him Kamal Hassain had made the blunder of showing a direct threat to Roger Stewart's bride, and once again the young Englishman acted with unthinking, bull-like impulse. His left hand moved in the gesture of a fast throw, as if to hurl the incriminating film away through the open bedroom window. Hassain made a frantic move to stop it before realizing that the film had not left Roger's hand, and in that off-balance moment he left himself wide open. Roger's right fist came up with violent fury and made an explosive crack against the side of the Egyptian's jaw.

The Inspector's head snappered backwards and his deep-set eyes glazed over as his shoulders slumped against the wall.

The blow had landed with perfect aim and timing and he was unconscious as he began to slide down the wall to the floor. Roger caught him beneath the armpits and lowered him silently, and then he turned to face Veronica who had gone pale.

"Roger," she whispered in horror. "What have you done?"

"Something I've been wanting to do all day," he returned in a low voice. And he rubbed his clenched fist with grim satisfaction. He looked down at the lolling head of Kamal Hassain, and then glanced at the outer door before he continued.

"And now let's get out of here. Those coppers waiting outside may not have heard the smack as I hit him, but now that the sound of his voice has stopped they'll soon guess that something's gone wrong."

He slipped the roll of film into his pocket as he murmured these words, and taking her arm he led her swiftly to the open window. They were on the third floor, but fortunately their room was at the back of the hotel, and ten feet below them lay an angle of the zigzag fire-escape. It took only a moment for Roger to help her climb over the window-sill, and then he lowered her at arms' length and dropped her neatly on to one of the broad steel rungs.

She waited as he swung one leg over the sill to follow her, and it was then that he heard a tentative knock on the outer door. It was followed by an enquiring voice in Arabic, obviously directed at the unconscious Inspector, and Roger knew that at any moment the two policemen stationed in the corridor would be bursting into the bedroom. The knowledge gave him extra momentum and he jumped hastily, grabbing at Veronica's arm and hustling her quickly down the fire-escape.

They were half way down when a startled shout of alarm told them that the waiting policemen had finally become impatient and discovered that their superior had been knocked out, and a second later a head popped through the window they had just left, bawling what was obviously Arabic for stop. Roger ignored it as he and Veronica clattered madly down the steel rungs, and together they jumped the last flight to the ground. They stumbled but kept going, and despite the frantic commands from behind they pelted across the hotel yard.

The two Egyptian policemen were cursing as they scrambled clumsily through the bedroom window and on to the fire-escape. They started in pursuit, still calling on the fleeing pair to halt, and one of them unslung his machine pistol and pointed it downwards. He hesitated as he attempted to track the running figures with its perforated muzzle, but they were already half way across the cobbled yard and before he could take proper aim they were dodging through the open gates into the back street beyond.

The policeman yelled an angry storm of Arabic as he lowered his gun, and then ran heavily down the fire-escape after his companion. They were puffing badly as they crossed the yard, but a crash of noise drew them directly to the dark mouth of an alley across the adjoining street. They could hear the fugitives running in the darkness ahead and quickly sprinted between the enclosing black walls. Seconds later they both tumbled over as their feet skidded through a mess of refuse from an overflowing bin that Roger had deftly twisted over in passing. They howled in fury as they rolled in the contents of the bin, but by the time they had struggled up and extricated themselves from the foul-smelling mess, the sound of running footsteps had faded and Roger and Veronica had escaped into the night.

* * *

For the next ten to fifteen minutes Roger and Veronica continued their blind, headlong flight. They twisted and turned through an endless succession of side streets and back alleys, stumbling over gutters and broken cobbles as they avoided all the main thoroughfares. Long after the sounds of their pursuers had died behind them the grip of panic thrust them along, and it was not until they were wholly spent and breathless that they at last slowed their hectic pace.

They had no energy left to immediately discuss their situation, and after resting briefly they moved on at a reduced rate. Roger was again limping, for the violent activity had re-awakened the throbbing of his badly bruised knee, and Veronica was looking very tired and defeated. The sky was brightening now, and once the first shades of grey had intruded into the night the dawn approached rapidly.

It was daylight when they eventually came out on to the wide road that ran parallel to the Nile, and the eastern sky was flushed with pink. They had emerged close to the 26th of July Bridge, and so they crossed the river to the long island of Gezira. They turned towards the tall landmark of the Cairo Tower, and after a few minutes found a secluded spot in one of the public gardens. Here they collapsed wearily on the grass behind a screen of low shrubs, and gradually revived their energies in the increasing warmth of the sun.

They had had an exhausting day and night, with no sleep in the past twenty-four hours except for the brief catnaps while travelling up from Luxor in the police car, but they were both young and healthy and after an hour they began to stir. By then there were plenty of people about, and Cairo was bustling with the business of the new day. Roger was able to buy iced drinks from an Arab vendor who had appeared with his barrow only a short distance away, and they emptied the bottles gratefully before they began to consider their next move.

Veronica said doubtfully. "I don't think you should have hit him, Roger. We're free now, but I don't see how it can help us in the long run."

Roger nodded glumly. "I know, but as he said that we'd be going to jail anyway it didn't seem as though we had anything to lose. I reckoned that if we could only get a breathing space in order to think, then we might find some way of getting out of Egypt. At the time anything was better than being shoved into separate cells for God knows how long."

She put her arms around his waist as they sat together on the grass, and her chestnut hair brushed his shoulder as she looked up at him. She said quietly.

"I can see that, darling. I don't want to be parted from you either. But how *are* we going to get out of Egypt? We have no passports, and no friends, and we daren't even go to the Embassy because that's sure to be the first place that they'll watch."

"I realized that," he admitted. "But there is a British Consulate at Alexandria, and when I hit the Inspector I had the idea that we might be able to get some help there. Either that or reach Port Said or Suez and try to sneak aboard some British ship going through the canal. We could have waited until the ship was at sea, and then thrown ourselves on the mercy of the master."

She looked at him hopefully. "Can we do either of those things?"

He hesitated, and then said reluctantly. "I'm not sure. Not any more. Both ideas seemed possible on the spur of the moment, and worth a try at least. But now that I've had time to think I can't see how we are going to get out of Cairo. There are only half a dozen roads out of the city, and the police are sure to have those and the railway station watched. We know now that this film that we're carrying is terribly important, and that they'll stop at nothing to get it back. So our chances of even getting out of Cairo appear to be nil, and even if we did slip through I think that damned Major would be smart enough to anticipate our movements and have all the ports watched. It's practically impossible to enter an airport and stow away aboard an aeroplane without help, so he knows that our only hope of getting out of the country is by sea."

"But if we can't get out of Cairo, what can we do? We've nowhere to go, and we're sure to be picked up if we wander the streets. By now every policeman in the city must know our descriptions and be on the lookout for us."

He nodded wearily. "It looks hopeless, doesn't it."

He was silent for a moment, and

then he tightened his arm around her shoulders until she looked up at his face.

"I'm sorry, Ronnie. Terribly sorry. This whole bloody mess is all my fault from start to finish. I should never have let that damned woman give me the film. I shouldn't have treated it so lightly at the start. And most definitely I shouldn't have tried to deny its existence to the police. I thought that by not admitting to anything I could avoid trouble, and all that I've done instead is to land us in a spot that's ten times worse than it would have been if we had told the truth when we were first questioned at Luxor."

"Anyone can be wise after the event," she replied softly. "So it's no use blaming yourself. I thought you were doing the right thing at Luxor, so it's not wholly your fault."

Roger smiled. "Dear Ronnie, if I'd blown up old Nasser himself and then stolen the pyramids I think you'd still stand by me!"

She found a smile. "Possibly. It may sound sad, but you're all I've got."

The first wave of despair was receding, and in another moment their natural humour might have borne them up. Veronica was still smiling but the smile vanished as Roger pulled her close and his lips clamped abruptly against her own. Her eyes went wide with alarm but he held her fast as he murmured.

"Don't look now, but there are two policemen coming this way."

Her body stiffened, but she responded to his embrace and neither of them dared to look up. The two Egyptian policemen in their white uniforms and black berets were strolling slowly along the path that was only ten yards away. They had their machine pistols dangling loosely from their shoulders and they gossiped vigorously as they passed. They paused in their conversation, and Roger felt his heart speed up with the knowledge that he was being watched. Then one of the Egyptians made a sly comment that drew a laugh from his companion, and they grinned back over their shoulders as they moved on.

Roger gave them another minute to get

out of sight beyond the lined trunks of some shading palms, and then he relaxed. He eased his grip and said quietly.

"They didn't suspect, but if they're on a regular beat we might not be so lucky next time. These shrubs half concealed us, but if we're still here when they come back they might decide to take a closer look."

She nodded in agreement. "Perhaps you're right. And now that the streets are full of people I think we'll be safer in the crowds. We ought to move."

Roger helped her to her feet, and somewhat nervously they returned to the road. They crossed through a spate of flying traffic, and then followed the bank of the Nile towards the Cairo Tower and the south end of Gezira Island. Across the broad blue river they could see the television building with its pylon mast, the red rooftops of the All Saints' Cathedral and then the great white block of the Nile Hilton with more giant hotels beyond Tahrir Bridge. Behind these latter hotels lay Garden City and the British Embassy, but they knew that to stray in that direction was akin to handing themselves tamely over to the police, so at the south end of Gezira they turned their backs on the east bank and crossed to the west.

They continued to walk slowly along the bank of the Nile, for whenever a policeman passed or danger seemed to threaten they could always lean over the embankment wall and pretend an absorbed interest in the far bank or the river below. They continued to discuss their situation, searching hopefully for a way out, and at last Veronica said.

"Roger, if you really think that the Major will be prepared for us to run north to Alex or Port Said, or due west to Suez, why don't we move south and go back down the Nile again. He won't expect us to do that."

"I suppose not," Roger acknowledged. "But what's the point? There's no way of escape south. There are no ports, and we couldn't cross into the Sudan without passports."

"I know. But if we can get to one of the larger towns down the Nile, Asyut or somewhere where we wouldn't be too noticeable, we could stay there for a few days until the hunt for us has died down. We might stand a better chance then of returning north."

Roger stopped and looked at her thoughtfully.

"Now that might be the answer. If we could get south for a few days, and then take a direct train right through to Alex or somewhere, then we might be able to get through Cairo without being spotted. The police will still be watching the station for us, but I doubt if they'll be searching every train coming up from the south. We can dodge them by already being on one of those trains with our tickets."

He paused, frowning, and then finished. "But we're still faced with the basic problem of getting out of Cairo in the first place. We dare not try and board a train at the station here, and it might be almost as dangerous trying to hitch a lift down the road."

She pointed behind him and said seriously.

"Why don't we take a boat?"

He twisted to look over the calm blue surface of the Nile. Directly opposite them a small felucca, the slant-masted craft of the Nile boatmen, was gliding past under full sail. Farther downstream moved a larger dhow, and in the distance, like misty scenes in a mirror from the past, moved two more slanted triangular sails. Roger watched them dubiously for a moment, and then the romance of the idea took a tentative grip on his mind. He turned back to Veronica and a gleam of excitement showed in his eye.

"I wonder," he mused. "Whether we could bribe some boatman to ferry us down the Nile."

"I don't see why not. If we can find a boat that's going down-river and then offer to pay our passage. We could make up some excuse that we're writing a book, or articles for a magazine. That should provide a reasonable explanation."

"Damnit, we'll try it." Roger decided abruptly. "One of these boatmen is sure to take us if we offer enough money. And fortunately I'm still wearing my money belt with all our cash and traveller's cheques."

"We've still got to change those into piastres," she reminded him. "And we won't be able to use a bank now that we have no passports."

"To hell with banks and piastres," he said cheerfully. "The black market rate is worth double the bank rate of exchange, and most shopkeepers have begged us to pay in sterling anyway. They'd rather have our money than their own, so I can't foresee any problems there."

Veronica smiled, remembering the shifty-eyed squads of Arabs who had flocked around them in the bazaar areas during their first two days in Cairo, all offering black market exchange rates for their sterling. She said; "Perhaps you're right. We've socked a policeman, resisted arrest, and endangered the security of the state, so we can hardly make matters worse by breaking the currency regulations." She linked her arm through his and finished. "Let's find ourselves a boat, before those horrible Hassain brothers find us."

They walked down the bank of the Nile for another hour before they found a suitable craft. Their choice was a medium sized dhow that was being loaded with oil drums from the back of a lorry that stood backed up to a small jetty. They watched the work, and waited at a distance until the lorry and its helpers drove away in a cloud of dust. Three men were left aboard the dhow, gossiping idly and tightening ropes, and Roger waited another hour or so until they showed signs of setting sail. Then at the last minute he approached the boat, reasoning that whatever the result of his request he had avoided any chance of the dhow's crew being able to gossip about it before they left.

The three Arabs, all dressed in flowing white gowns and ragged turbans gathered round with interest as he outlined his demand. Only the boat's owner spoke a smattering of English, and that amounted mostly to "*Yas sah*" and "*No sah*," but gradually he began to understand. The three brown faces flickered from happy grins to looks of doubt and perplexity, more grins, arguments, and then back through the whole range again. Roger persevered patiently, and managed to establish that they were taking the oil drums down the river, and that their destination was a town called Beni Suef, which he knew to be about sixty-five miles south. It was ideal for his purpose, for it was a reasonably large town and the distance was about right, neither too near nor too far, but he still had to persuade the three Arabs to take them as passengers.

Quite abruptly he realized why his request appeared to be failing, for in his anxiety to determine where the dhow was headed he had forgotten to mention money. He dug into his shirt to open his money belt, and produced two five-pound sterling notes. The Arabs immediately became eager and argued vehemently amongst themselves. Their captain finally faced Roger and indicated that the ten pounds was only sufficient for one passenger. It would be another ten pounds for two.

Roger knew that the wily old Arab

had guessed that they had some urgent need for wishing to travel on the dhow but he was in no position to argue. On principle he bargained for a little longer, for he sensed that it would be unwise to let his shrewd opponent realize how desperate their need was, and then he gracefully gave in. The old Arab accepted the four five-pound notes with a beaming grin that showed up the black gaps between his teeth, and showed them to his companions, who were apparently his sons, before stuffing them carefully inside his robes.

Roger and Veronica were shown a place to sit under a tiny canvas awning that sheltered the only part of the deck that was not stacked with the black oil drums, and from there they watched as the dhow was got under way. The great lateen sail was unfurled from the soaring mast, and slowly the craft pushed out into the river. A gentle wind crackled the sail as the prow turned downstream, and the dhow drifted like some living thing stirring lazily to life, reluctant to awaken to the full blazing sun above.

Roger looked at Veronica and she returned his smile, and for this moment at least they forgot their troubles. They did not know what further trials awaited them, or what would be the outcome, but they had won a respite in which to plan and think, and temporarily that was enough.

11

The Net Draws Tighter

That same afternoon, as Roger and Veronica enjoyed the timeless scenery of their passage down the Nile, Schererzade received her second visit from Faizal Hassain. It was now five days since she had been struck down, and although her body showed signs that it would mend, her mental worry was still keeping her weak and ill. She had suffered a relapse after the Major's first visit, and her nerves were almost continually on edge. Her doctors had refused her any further visitors, and for that she was glad. But when Hassain appeared again at her bedside she realized that the security Major made his own rules.

Hassain smiled at her. "You look pale, my dear, but I hope that despite that you will soon recover. The customers miss you at the *Ali Baba*. Moshe has hired a new dancer to fill your place in the cabaret, but I am afraid that she cannot twirl her navel quite so enticingly as you. She is merely a professional, while you were an artiste."

He bowed his head towards the large bouquet of flowers in the vase by her bedside, ignoring her frightened eyes as he inhaled with pleasure.

"Such fragrance. And expensive too. One assumes that they must be a gift from your lover, the good Colonel Mehran?"

A muscle trembled in Schererzade's throat, but this time he was waiting for a reply and she forced herself to speak.

"Yes, they are from Hamid."

Hassain plucked one of the blooms and held it sadly between his fingers. "Poor Hamid Mehran. The noble Colonel could have been one of Egypt's finest officers — if it were not for his foolish blindness where you are concerned. Now his downfall is assured, and his honour is ruined."

He smiled again, and gently crushed the flower in his closing fist. Equally as casually he opened his hand again, and allowed the scattering of bruised petals to drift down on to Schererzade's pillow.

The dancer flinched, twisting her head away from the touch of a petal that had wafted on to her cheek. When she moved a spasm of pain shot from the region of her cracked pelvis, and tiny beads of sweat appeared around her tightening mouth. She forced herself to lie still, and once again her eyes were drawn towards the face of Faizal Hassain. She knew that he had come to play with her, to gloat over her and enjoy his own twisted brand of mental sadism. But she had to ask the question he expected.

"What — what has happened to Hamid? Have you arrested him?"

"Not yet." Hassain reached for the petal on her cheek and gently brushed it away. "But I think that soon I shall."

Schererzade closed her eyes and asked. "Then why have you come?"

"Out of kindness." Hassain smiled. "I thought that perhaps you would be interested to know what is happening in the great, busy world beyond your bedroom window. The most important thing, perhaps, is that I have found the young English couple who came to your assistance when you suffered your — er — accident! Their name is Stewart, a very impetuous and foolish young man with a wife to match. I do not know what request you made of them, but I do know that the object you passed on was a roll of 35 millimetre film, and that they still have this film in their possession."

Schererzade lay stiff, her eyes still closed, saying nothing. However, her face was showing more traces of breaking sweat. Hassain's eyes were glittering, and he moved the sheets that covered her, and pressed his large brown hand to her thin nightdress beneath her left breast.

"I seem to have alarmed you," he purred softly. "Your heart is beating at an almost dangerous rate." He chuckled as she pushed his hand away, and then withdrew. "Perhaps I should have added that for the moment these young people have managed to escape me. But the fact that they are still loose is irrelevant, for they cannot hope to stay free for long. Every road is blocked to ensure that they cannot leave Cairo, and as the police and my agents are making a thorough search of the city I expect to hear at any moment that Mr Stewart and his young wife have been recaptured."

Schererzade's eyes screwed tighter, suppressing her anguish, and Hassain went on.

"We are watching the British Embassy of course, but I think that even they will have the sense to anticipate that. In their position I can only see one course of action, and that is for them to attempt to reach Alexandria, Port Said or Suez and there try to buy a passage out of Egypt. So the police of those cities have been notified, even though I doubt if our quarry can ever get that far. Their position is hopeless — and so is yours."

Schererzade opened her eyes. Her nerves were shredded but there was still a tiny flicker of fight in her mind. She said feebly.

"The film is not all that important. The photographs are merely of aircraft at one of the Air Force bases in northern Egypt. They are not generally publicized, but not really top secret. The film is not worth all your trouble."

She faltered and her eyes flickered towards Hassain. He was regarding her with interest and showed no signs of interrupting, and she drew fresh breath and went on.

"I bribed one of the young officers at the *Ali Baba* to take the pictures, and they were nothing to do with Hamid Mehran. There is nothing that you can hold against him. As for this English couple, they are mere tourists. I told them to throw the film away. That is all. They are foolish if they think that they are running away with something that is important." She coughed, and her throat jerked convulsively before she finished. "I am a spy. I will admit that. I will stand up in court and say it. But only of small things. There is no need for you to try and persecute others simply to bring a charge against me. Is — is that not enough?"

The Major looked down at her with an expression of mock regret. He was silent for one long, unbearable minute, and then he answered softly.

"No, it is not enough. For apart from the confession that you are a spy, which I knew anyway, I believe none of it. You see, three men, whom I must assume to be Israeli agents, have already made one attempt to kidnap our young friends in the temples of Karnak, and they would hardly take such blatant risks in order to gain some simple pictures of our unpublicized aircraft. And besides, I have been conducting some quiet enquiries concerning Colonel Hamid Mehran. I know the nature of the project on which your lover is working, and I know that he has been freely handling the documents involved. I suspect that those are the secrets that your roll of film betrays, and if I am correct I shall have you shot."

He straightened up, savouring the sick consternation in her eyes, and casually he helped himself to another bloom from Mehran's bouquet. He fixed it in the lapel of his dark suit, and gave her a parting smile.

"Goodbye, Scheerzade. For now I

have work to do. May Allah smile upon my efforts, and bring sweetness to your dreams."

She watched him leave, and only then did a sob escape her as she lay back upon her pillows. She knew that the net was drawing ever tighter around her, but that there was absolutely nothing that she could do about it while her broken body fastened her helplessly to her bed. She was trapped like a fallen butterfly pinned to a paper, awaiting only the final jab of the collector's needle through her body.

Her only hope was that Shabetai might catch up with the young English couple before Faizal Hassain, but since that first visit she had received no word from the Israeli. Where, she wondered desperately, was Shabetai now?

★ ★ ★

The answer was less than a mile away, for Shabetai and his two companions had returned to Cairo. They had travelled up from Luxor by car after finding out that Roger and Veronica had been whisked away by the Cairo police, and now they occupied a back room in a small café near the Khan El Khalili market, one of the old quarters of Cairo. Zadek and Ayoub sat at a small table, sipping from glasses of sweetened mint tea, and holding hands like shy lovers, while behind them Shabetai was engaged with the telephone affixed to the wall.

The telephone call was coming from a public booth near Tahrir Square, and the caller was a small, nervous-eyed police sergeant named Barrani. Barrani worked in the police department building, close to the office of Kamal Hassain, but unbeknown to that astute young Inspector he was also in the habit of making a little cash on the side by passing any useful information on to the Israelites.

Shabetai listened carefully to all that Barrani had to say, assured the man that he would be paid in due course, and then issued some emphatic instructions. Barrani's tone became wheedling, but at last he agreed to what was wanted and Shabetai rang off. The slim Israeli looked grimly pleased as he turned away from the phone, and his weak eyes gleamed behind his steel-rimmed glasses. Zadek and Ayoub looked towards him enquiringly.

"There is news," Shabetai announced. "The young Englishman and his wife have escaped from the police, and they still have the film in their possession. At the moment the whole of the Egyptian police force is looking for them, but the moment any clue to their whereabouts reaches Police Headquarters my informer has promised to call and let me know. So we must have a fast car waiting at all times, for when the call comes through we will be racing against Faizal Hassain and the police. Our chance of success is small, but it is a chance and we must be prepared to take it. Do you understand?"

Zadek nodded, and somewhat sadly his brown fingers ceased their slow caressing movement along the back of Ayoub's hand. "I understand," he said. "I will attend to the car."

12

A Stroke of Luck

The slow, dreamy journey up the Nile took seventeen hours. There was very little wind and mostly they chugged along under the power of the dhow's battered auxiliary engine, which was cared for by the old Arab's eldest son. There were no stops along the way and they kept going throughout the blistering hot afternoon, and then through the cool of the night beneath a majestic, star-embellished sky. A light breeze sprang up to give mysterious life to the rustling fronds of the countless palms that lined the silent banks; the Nile tinkled and murmured as it brushed smoothly against the dhow's hardwood hull, and the slanting, creaking mast, its sail sagging wistfully in the hope that the breeze would strengthen, made a fantasy stairway to the vivid night sky, the realm of Khonsu, the hawk-headed God of the moon and the son of Ammon Ra.

For Roger and Veronica it was a blessed opportunity to rest and to restore their flagging energies. At first they had to return the chattering attempts at conversation from their hosts, but the language difficulty soon proved too large a barrier, and they were finally reduced to exchanging shrugs and grins. The two younger Arabs seemed disappointed that their curiosity about their two strange passengers could not be satisfied, but they remembered the money that their father had stuffed inside his grubby robes and stayed philosophically cheerful.

The sun-bleached deck of the dhow was not a perfect bed, but Roger and Veronica managed to doze through most of the night. At dusk they were invited by the old Arab to share the food that one of his sons had prepared, and at dawn they were awakened with a similar invitation. Each meal was composed simply of flat, pancake-like loaves of coarse bread, each one cut into four, slit up the middle, and then filled with a mixture of cooked meat and pieces of fish. It was not an appetizing repast, for the pan in which the scraps of meat and fish had sizzled was thick with grease and black with years of use, but Roger and Veronica were both hungry and accepted gratefully on each occasion.

After the second meal they stayed awake, sitting on the deck with their backs against some of the lashed oil drums, and watching the blood-red eye of the sun slowly peeping through the bright green crowns of the date palms along the eastern bank. The temperature was very pleasant now, and they were able to enjoy the gentle movement of the dhow. They passed several of the smaller, faster feluccas, gliding gracefully over the silver-white, early-morning calmness of the Nile. As the sun rose the river turned gradually to blue.

All too soon it seemed, the dusty town of Beni Suef appeared on the west bank ahead, and they realized regretfully that their idle pleasure cruise was almost over. It had left them strengthened and refreshed, but so far they still had no definite plans beyond waiting here until the hue and cry in Cairo had had a chance to die down, and then attempting to head north again to Port Said or Alexandria.

The sun was perhaps half way to noon as the dhow manoeuvred lethargically against another short jetty. Roger and Veronica stood upright, out of the way, and watched as the old Arab took the tiller and his sons made ready with the mooring ropes. Another pair of grinning brown men in scruffy turbans and long robes had appeared on the jetty to help, and the dhow was soon lashed into place. The crew scrambled quickly to furl the big sail that had been only partially responsible for their progress, and then it was time to go ashore.

Roger thanked the old Arab boatman, and then shook hands with both him and his sons. Veronica repeated the gesture, and after a final jabber of parting words, which neither side really understood, they were able to take their leave and walk away. The crew of the dhow continued to grin and waved to them until they were out of sight.

They found that Beni Suef, the capital of this province of Upper Egypt, was a reasonably large town, over twice the size of Luxor, the only other Egyptian town they had seen. As they walked through its streets they were pestered by a gang of urchins yelling *"Baksheesh! Baksheesh!"* but constant begging was something they had become accustomed to in Cairo and Roger waved them away. The sun was getting hotter and they sought out a café and bought iced drinks, which they found they needed continually through the heat of the day. Here they faced up to the situation, and tried to plan what they would do for the next few days until they felt that it was safe enough to return north.

Roger still had ten pounds in sterling and fifty pounds in travellers' cheques in the money belt around his waist, so they had no immediate financial worries. Their main problem lay in finding somewhere to stay, for although they could afford a hotel Roger was unwilling to try and book a room without passports. Most hoteliers would want to check their identity, and without the evidence of passports might be suspicious enough to call the police. They brooded glumly, and then decided that the only safe course was to avoid hotels and sleep out in one of the town's parks for the next few nights.

Their next problem was the fact that they were completely without baggage, for they had escaped from the Hotel Saladin with only their clothes and the troublesome roll of film that Roger had slipped hastily into his pocket. Veronica was of the somewhat bitter opinion that they should throw the latter away, but now that he knew something of its value Roger had determined to hang on to it in the hope that he could ultimately pass it on to the British authorities somewhere. This was what he had originally undertaken to do, and he felt that if he could still achieve that one small triumph he would at least have saved something from the mess he had made. Veronica was inclined to dispute the fact, but he steered her away from the subject by pointing out that her nose was shiny and that he could still afford to buy her a new powder compact and lipstick, together with a few other basic necessities.

They left the café with renewed spirits and after wandering aimlessly for a while found their way to the equivalent of Cairo's bazaar area. Here they slowed their pace even more until approached by the inevitable oily-tongued shopkeeper who invited them to inspect his wares. They went into his dark cavern of a shop, and first the man showed them a large range of pungent smelling perfumes which they declined. Next, in a hushed, confidential whisper, he tried to sell them a highly exotic paste, a recipe handed down through the centuries from the temple priests of Ancient Egypt, and sworn to warm their blood, revitalize their youth, and stimulate their sexual appetite. Again they declined, although this time they were smiling. Finally, the shopkeeper came to his third line of business, which as they had hoped was a little black-market money-changing, and they began to do business.

Roger ultimately changed two of his ten-pound travellers' cheques, the exchange rate was less than for actual sterling because the cheques were less easily negotiable, but because his sterling was easier to change Roger had decided to hold on to it as long as possible. For his two cheques he received thirty-five Egyptian pounds which amounted to three thousand five hundred piastres, and he was satisfied that they could make that sum last for a long time yet. He also felt obliged to buy a small bottle of perfume, but insisted that he could still manage without the sex paste.

Veronica was still chuckling when they got outside.

"Perhaps we should have bought some," she said. "We could always save it for a rainy day when you might need it."

Roger grinned at her. "By the time I get old enough to need any artificial aids, you'll be so old you'll be glad I've stopped."

"Braggart," she accused him. "I bet I

last longer than you do!"

Their good humour was with them again and they set off happily on their miniature shopping spree.

First they bought themselves a decorated leather carrying-bag, for there were a great variety of these on display as souvenirs for the tourists and they were reasonably cheap. Then they bought a change of underclothes, socks, towels and the few toilet articles they needed. Veronica bought herself fresh cosmetics and hair brushes and pronounced herself twice as happy. By then it was past noon and they were getting hungry again, so they set about looking for somewhere to eat.

Most of the Egyptian restaurants they peered into were cheap places with a repelling aspect. They buzzed with flies, and the steaming food pans just inside the door looked anything but inviting. Veronica wrinkled her nose at each one in turn, and they continued to search for an establishment of higher class. Finally they found a large hotel near the Nile and went inside to search for the dining room.

A Nubian waiter with a red tarbosh and baggy trousers directed them into a cool restaurant that obviously catered for tourists, and thankfully they sat down. The large menu boasted an excellent selection and they both ordered large omelettes and salads, and more iced lemonade. While they waited for their order they relaxed contentedly, and Roger noticed that there were three young men in faded jeans and brightly coloured, open-necked shirts at the next table. The trio were talking cheerfully over their meal, and their slightly gutteral accents told him that they were Germans.

Their food arrived and Roger and Veronica ate heartily. The omelettes were beautifully done, and after the rough fare on the dhow they enjoyed them all the more. They finished with large dishes of ice cream and expressed their satisfaction as they relaxed over coffee. Their conversation had lulled, and it was then that Roger felt a polite tap on his shoulder.

"Excuse me — " It was one of the young Germans from the next table, blonde and blue-eyed with a friendly smile. He was tilting his chair back on two legs to lean across the gap between the tables. "Excuse me, but you are English, yes?"

Roger nodded, and admitted that they were.

"Ah, that is good. I am talking the right language." The German's smile flashed wider as he spoke. "My companions are wondering if perhaps you have come up from Luxor? We are going south down the Nile, and we wish to know the condition of the road?"

"It's a pretty good road," Roger said hesitantly. He wasn't going to add that they had travelled it in a police car and went on. "It runs beside the railway in a lot of places and the surface looks reasonable."

"Ah, so you are travelling by train. They tell me that the trains here are worse than those in India. Is it true?"

Roger grinned. "I haven't actually done any train journeys in India, but I think it must be. The Indian trains certainly can't be any worse."

"If they are, then I don't want to know about them." Veronica added. "There's nothing worse than an all night train journey with a dozen Arabs squabbling in your lap."

The remaining two Germans were taking an interest and seemed pleased to be able to talk. One of them asked.

"You are returning now to Cairo?"

Roger nodded. "Yes, but we're staying here a couple of days first."

"Staying here?" The blonde man showed surprise. "But why break your journey here? There is nothing in Beni Suef."

It was an awkward question, but Veronica found an answer.

"That's why we've stopped," she said. "We thought we'd like to see what an ordinary Egyptian town was like, one with no monuments and no swarms of guides."

Roger registered agreement, and then tactfully changed the subject. "When you get to Luxor, don't miss the Karnak temples," he said. "They really are the highlight of the trip."

"Ah, but we do not go first to Luxor," the German explained. "We go only as far as Quena, which is just before you get to Luxor, and then we go to Quseir. It is a port on the Red Sea, and there we will rest and do lots of swimming. But we will make a visit to Luxor on the way back."

One of his companions added. "We have been seven days in Cairo, so a little holiday by the sea will be very pleasant. Also we hope to hire a boat, and perhaps do some fishing."

The three Germans continued to converse in a friendly fashion, confiding their plans and exchanging impressions of Cairo and Egypt. All three were engineering students from Munich, and they had travelled across Europe and then through Turkey and the Middle East in a Volkswagen Minibus, and like most young travellers they showed a great keenness for swapping tales. Veronica responded to their reminiscences with enthusiasm, but for the moment Roger's brain was ticking over with the first glimmering of a new idea as the conversation flowed around him. He waited for the blonde leader of the trio to finish telling how they had shipped the Minibus from Beirut to Port Said, and then deftly brought them back to the subject of Quseir.

"You mentioned the Red Sea and fishing," he remarked. "Now I wouldn't mind trying my hand at that. In fact we did hope to get across to Quseir for a few days when we came away from Luxor, but unfortunately there's no railway line." He was aware of Veronica giving him a sudden puzzled stare, and hoped that the Germans would not notice her as he continued quickly. "I used to do a lot of pike-fishing back in England. Pike are the biggest freshwater fish we've got, and I've always wanted to have a go at something bigger. A couple of days shark-fishing in the Red Sea would be just ideal."

"I do not think we will try to catch anything as dangerous as sharks." The speaker was the one who had first introduced the subject of fishing. Like their leader he was blonde and blue-eyed, but he was slimmer and wore spectacles. He laughed easily and added. "But shark-fishing should be possible for those with more ambition."

The leader of the trio hesitated for a moment, and then he looked at Roger.

"You would really like to make a visit to Quseir?"

Roger nodded. "If there had been a railway line we would definitely have gone. But there isn't and we just couldn't afford to hire a car."

The German looked back at his companions. "What do you think? We have the room?"

The blonde youth in the spectacles nodded, and the darker youth on his right said cheerfully.

"It will perhaps be a squeeze, but I think we can manage."

"Sure, we can manage." The leader of the three turned back to Roger. "If you wish to come with us we can take you to Quseir. Perhaps you will be squashed because we have a lot of baggage in the Minibus, but I think it will not be too bad. We shall stay three days by the sea,

206

perhaps four, and then you can return with us as far as Quena where you can get the train back to Cairo. What do you think?"

Roger tried not to look as though he had been hoping for such an offer, and pretended a little uncertainty.

"It's very good of you to ask us," he wavered. "But are you sure you've got the room? We don't want to put you to any trouble."

"It's no trouble," the German insisted. He grinned broadly. "We three have been travelling for several weeks now, and we get a little tired of each other's company. It will be good to have some new faces to talk to for a few days. Also it helps us to maintain our English."

"Well in that case — " Roger looked at Veronica. "What do you think, Ronnie? There's not really much to see here in Beni Suef, and I'd rather give the place a miss and see Quseir."

There was a blankness in her dark hazel eyes that showed that she completely failed to understand, but characteristically she smiled and gave him full support.

"If that's okay with you, I'm perfectly happy."

"Then it is settled," said the blonde German. "You must come with us." He smiled and added. "If we are to travel together then we should know each other's names. I am Kurt, and my friends are Ernst and Walter."

His two companions nodded in acknowledgement. The second blonde youth with the spectacles was Ernst, and the darker one was Walter. Roger introduced himself and Veronica and they shook hands all round before Kurt suggested that they might as well get on their way. Roger agreed, and made up a false story that they had only just got off the train to explain why they still had no baggage with them. The fact that they had nothing more substantial than the lightly-filled carrying bag did not seem to arouse any suspicion, and Kurt called cheerfully for the waiter to bring their bills.

A few minutes later they walked out of the hotel restaurant, with the three Germans moving ahead to lead the way to their Minibus. Veronica seized her opportunity to drag Roger back for a moment and eyed him severely.

"Roger, what on earth are we supposed to be doing?" she demanded helplessly. "You've never shown any previous interest in fishing and I don't think you've ever caught a pike in all your life. In fact I doubt if you could even tell a fishing rod from a telegraph pole. Yet now, all of a sudden you want to go fishing for sharks in the Red Sea. It's crazy! What are you up to?"

"Well I'm not exactly going to look for sharks," he said wryly. "It simply occurred to me that Quseir would be a better place for us to lie low than here in Beni Suef. For a start it's much more remote from Cairo, and also we'll be less noticeable there. As it's on the sea we shall have the excuse of swimming and fishing to explain our presence, while here there are no real tourist attractions and after a couple of days of walking the streets we'll begin to stick out like sore thumbs."

Her lips made a slight, doubtful pout.

"It sounds sensible, but did you have to commit us to fishing for sharks?"

"Well I had to pretend an interest in something, and besides, I had a sort of idea. A wild one maybe, but it might be worthy a try."

She gave him an even more doubtful look, and asked.

"What sort of wild idea?"

"Well — " he hedged a moment. "The Red Sea is pretty narrow, only about two hundred miles wide, and there's a constant stream of shipping flowing through it from Suez. I thought that if we could hire a boat we could pretend to go fishing and simply sail out as far as possible and look out for a ship heading south to Aden. If we could get one to pick us up we can always pretend engine trouble, or bash a hole through the bottom just before they come alongside. If we could strike lucky and get landed at Aden then all our troubles will be over."

Veronica shook her head and said bluntly.

"It sounds just too wild to me."

"Maybe, but if it doesn't work out we

can still come back to Quena after four days with the Germans, and then book a straight through ticket to Alexandria on the train as we planned. Meanwhile it'll at least be more fun making pseudo-fishing trips from Quseir than it will be prowling the streets of this miserable place. Either way you look at it, meeting Kurt and his friends is a stroke of damned good luck."

Veronica shrugged her shoulders resignedly.

"A short holiday by the sea is fine," she said. "But as for thumbing a lift on the high seas I think my beloved Lord and Master has had a bit too much of old Ammon Ra up there!"

Roger grinned and took her firmly by the arm.

"Don't argue, beautiful slave. I have already commanded. And if we don't hurry the German boys might go without us."

At that moment Kurt came back to look for them and they made their apologies as they hurried out to the waiting Minibus.

13

By the Red Sea

Roger's opinion that their chance meeting with the three Germans was a stroke of luck held more truth than he realized, for shortly after they had left Beni Suef the old boatman who had brought them down the Nile reported their presence to the local police. It was not that he wished them ill, but simply that he was a shrewd and careful man, and that he knew that in Colonel Gamal Nasser's new United Arab Republic it was always best to report everything to the police. However, Roger and Veronica were unaware of what was taking place behind them, and settled down to enjoy the ride and cement their new-found friendship.

The blonde Kurt drove the Minibus, handling the wheel confidently as though he had spent all his life whizzing through groves of date palms and mud-walled villages. He dodged groups of shuffling fellahin, potholes, donkeys, camels and bullock-drawn carts all with equal accuracy, and still managed to devote most of his attention to the conversation around him. Ernst sat on his right, while Walter sat in the back with their two extra passengers, surrounded by rolled-up sleeping bags and a jungle of camping and cooking equipment.

It was another hot and dusty trip, but with lively company it was much more bearable than the drive up from Luxor in the police car two days previously. They stopped for iced drinks more frequently, and during the hottest part of the afternoon Kurt pulled up on the bank of the Nile and all five cooled off by going swimming. Roger was able to borrow a spare pair of shorts from Walter, while Veronica dived in quickly in her bra and briefs.

The river was warm and clean, and they splashed around for an hour before they dressed and returned to the Minibus. The welcome break had left them much refreshed, and Kurt drove on almost non-stop for the next four hours when they passed through Asyut at about six o'clock. Here Ernst relieved him for the next fifty miles or so, and by then they were hungry enough to need another meal. They made their second stop in a shady palm grove and Walter capably cooked up some canned soups and stewing beef on a large primus. They had gathered by now that Walter was in charge of stores and catering; Kurt maintained and drove the Minibus; while Ernst acted as co-driver, navigator and anything else that was required.

When they pushed on again it was getting dark, and the rush of air that came through the open windows became more like a breeze, rather than the fiery breath of some medieval dragon. They continued south down the Nile road until nearly midnight, when Kurt called a final halt a few miles north of Quena. The night was so mild that it was not even necessary to pitch a tent, and the three Germans simply unrolled their sleeping bags on the soft sand by the roadside and slept under the stars. Roger and Veronica were able to stretch out upon some spare blankets in the back of the Minibus, and so all five passed a peaceful night.

They were on the road again early the next morning, for Kurt hoped to complete the last stage of the journey before the full heat of mid-day. They drove through Quena, and here they turned away from the Nile Valley to follow the old caravan route across the foot of the Arabian desert to the Red Sea. Here there was no shady chain of feathered palm trees, and no green irrigated fields of grain or cotton. Instead the desert became a grim reality on either side.

Walter remarked somewhat quietly that a previous party of German tourists had died on this route only a few weeks before. Their car had run off the hard road and stuck in the soft sand. The unfortunate occupants had been unable to dig it free, and they had not had sufficient water to last them until they were ultimately found. This harsh fact gave them all a firm respect for their surroundings, and Kurt handled the wheel with an unusual amount of care and concentration.

However, despite Walter's cautionary warning they suffered no mishaps, and after a further four hours of driving they rolled thankfully into Quseir. They had passed several small Bedouin camps and villages on the way that had given an added interest to their journey, but there was nothing to compare with their first inviting glimpse of the Red Sea.

Almost immediately a problem arose, for although Roger had expected that the Germans would be camping on the beach, they had in fact elected to stop at a hotel, and naturally they expected that he and Veronica would be joining them. Roger had to explain that they had no passports, and made up the weak excuse that they had inadvertently left them with the bulk of their luggage in their hotel room in Cairo.

Kurt listened, frowning, and then gave a casual shrug of his shoulders.

"I think it will not matter," he said. "Just as long as you can remember all the details from your passports so that the man at the desk can write them all down in his book. These Egyptians do not care who you are, just as long as all their silly paper work is filled in."

"Well I know most of it," Roger said doubtfully. "But I can't remember the passport numbers."

"Put down any number," Ernst told him cheerfully. "They won't know the difference. If the right column is filled with figures they will be satisfied. All these countries are the same. You have to fill in forms, forms, forms all the time. And no one ever reads them. As long as something is scribbled in all the blank spaces they are happy."

Roger hesitated reluctantly, for he could hardly admit that if the hotelier was not satisfied then the police might come rushing round with a warrant for their arrest. But without explaining the truth it was going to be difficult to deter their new friends. Kurt slapped him on the shoulder and said jovially.

"You come with us. If there is any argument and you cannot stay in the hotel without your passports, then you will have to use the Minibus, or borrow our tent. But first we will try the hotel and see what happens."

In the face of such obvious logic Roger could see no way of refusing, and so he decided to take the risk. All five of them climbed out of the Minibus and Kurt led the way into the small hotel.

The three Germans booked a room with no difficulty, but when it came to Roger's turn there was an awkward moment. The Egyptian desk clerk was a bossy, officious youth, and when he learned that Roger and Veronica could not produce their passports his dark brown face showed blank refusal. It was impossible, he protested in stumbling English. Utterly impossible. Visitors must show their passports! He was still protesting excitably when Kurt calmly took the registration book away from him, twisted it round, and pushed it in front of Roger.

"Here," he said. "Fill in all the details. It will be all right. It will be all right," he repeated, brushing aside the frantic babbling of the clerk. "Everything will be filled in properly. There will be no trouble."

Roger faltered for a second, and then picked up a pen and boldly filled in the relative columns with their names, nationality, dates and places of birth, and all the other details demanded. Those he could not remember he made up. He wrote swiftly while Kurt continued to placate the anguished clerk, and signed his name with a flourish. He smiled confidently and returned the book.

The Egyptian quietened a little, and read the new entries dubiously. He still resented the way matters had been taken out of his hands, and stressed petulantly that the details should be checked against a passport. Roger sensed, however, that he was on the winning side now that the entries had actually been made, and tactfully produced a hundred piastre note to soothe the desk clerk's ruffled pride. The youth dithered a little more, but finally gave way. Kurt gave Roger a comradely grin, and now that the matter was settled they all returned to the

219

Minibus to fetch their baggage.

A few moments later they were shown to their rooms on the second floor of the hotel. The three Germans were given one large room with three single beds, while Roger and Veronica were offered a double room farther along the corridor. Theirs was not an elaborate room, being simply furnished with a large bed and wardrobe, but it boasted an adjoining bath and shower, and that was the only thing that was important. They thanked the Egyptian desk clerk, who was still a little nettled, and smiled their satisfaction in order to avoid antagonizing him any further.

When he had left them they were alone for the first time since they had eaten in Beni Suef twenty-four hours ago, and the door had barely closed before they relaxed in each other's arms. They kissed fondly and it was some time before they broke apart. Veronica sighed and said.

"I needed that. Everything's become so wild and crazy that it's nice to get back to natural habits."

Roger smiled. "The pace should settle

down a bit now. We'll buy some new swimming costumes and spend the afternoon on the beach. We needn't start looking for a fishing boat till tomorrow."

Veronica nodded, and then looked at him with a flicker of doubt.

"Are you sure that nasty little desk clerk won't go to the police about our not having any passports?"

Roger frowned. "I don't think he will. Now that we're actually here he'll have to admit that we bullied him into not doing his job properly. The story doesn't show him in a very noble light, so I think he'll keep it to himself."

"Even so, you took a chance."

"I know," he admitted. "But what else could I do. The only alternative was to tell Kurt and the others our true story, and I don't want to do that. I know they would offer to help us — they're three good types — but I don't want them to become any more deeply involved than they are already. At the moment they don't know the true facts, and so they have an honest plea of ignorance as their defence if the police should ever find out that they have helped us. They can't be charged with knowingly aiding our escape, and that's the way I want it to stay."

Veronica had listened seriously and now said. "You're right, of course you are! I hadn't got round to thinking it out yet, but I can see that the less that we tell Kurt and the boys then the better it will be for them. We can't solve our troubles by spreading them on to other people, and even if we did confide I don't see how they can help us any more than they have done."

Roger smiled, for although he disliked the feeling that he was deceiving the three friendly Germans, he was glad to have Veronica's support in maintaining their silence. He showed his appreciation by kissing her once more, and she approved with wholehearted response. When she drew back she said.

"That was nice. Now let's stop worrying about our problems. Right now I'm feeling all hot and sweaty instead of my dainty, ladylike self, and that shower looks like heaven. Unzip me, darling, and then find me a towel."

Roger turned her round and unzipped her, and then carried their bag across to the bed and began to spread out its few contents. When he looked back with the soap and towel he found that she had already laid aside her dress and bra, and was then stepping absently out of her pantie briefs. He smiled and flicked the towel smartly before she could straighten up with a wincing yelp.

"Beast!" she cried indignantly.

"Shameless temptress," he responded cheerfully. "I'll do even more beastly things to you if you continue to stand there in your glorious birthday suit."

"Big, adorable beast," she modified, and dodged another playful cut with the towel as she slipped away.

Roger's blood raced as her laughing, naked figure vanished behind the shower curtain. He heard the rush of running water, and a few moments later he joined her beneath the exhilarating spray. They embraced breathlessly, wetly, eagerly; and he realized almost painfully that it was two whole days since they had last shared the love-making that was ordained to follow.

★ ★ ★

That afternoon they spent with the three Germans on the beach, the time passing in a lazy round of swimming and simply basking in the hot sun. In the evening they idly explored Quseir, famous for an old fort built by the armies of Napoleon, and for the even older fact that it had been an ancient embarkation point for Moslem pilgrims wishing to cross the Red Sea to Mecca. The day ended over an excellent meal of fresh caught crayfish at the hotel, and they lingered over a bottle of wine with Kurt, Ernst and Walter before finally retiring for the night.

When they came down the following morning they found the three Germans in the hotel yard, tinkering with their Minibus. Kurt, dressed simply in shorts and with streaks of grease in his blond hair, was working on the engine, while

Ernst and Walter stood by like attendant nurses to a capable surgeon. Roger offered his assistance, but as they were merely keeping up some routine maintenance the offer was cheerfully declined, and so he and Veronica bade them a temporary goodbye.

They walked down to the beach, and now that their companions were likely to be busy for most of the morning Roger considered it an opportune time to enquire after a fishing boat. Veronica was still dubious about the whole idea, but she had to admit that they could do no harm by trying. The period of relaxation they were enjoying had restored them both to good spirits and Roger was in an optimistic mood.

There was a variety of craft in and around the harbour, mostly dhows with tall swaying masts, but a few of them were fitted, like the one that had carried them down the Nile, with ancient auxiliary engines. These latter ones interested Roger, and he approached a group of turbaned, long-robed boatmen who were pulling over their nets, and attempted to make his requirements known. At first there was misunderstanding, and one shrivel-faced old patriarch tried to sell him some large red crabs. Another offered them a wriggling baby squid, grinning as he held it towards Veronica's recoiling nose, but finally they shouted for a young Arab boy of about twelve who came trotting quickly towards them. The boy had a lively grin and a small smattering of English.

With the aid of their juvenile interpreter Roger managed to explain that they wished to do their own fishing. The men jabbered unintelligibly, but their nodding heads and eager smiles made his optimism soar. He was confident that everything was going to go right.

The crash came when he realized that although he could hire practically any small fishing boat in the harbour, hiring the boat would also entail hiring its owner. They were all willing to take him fishing, but not to let him take one of their fishing boats out alone. He argued helplessly, but they were unshakeable. They could not understand why he would wish to go fishing alone, and each one insisted that if his boat was hired then naturally he would have to go along to sail it.

Roger finally gave up the unequal struggle and extricated himself as well as he could. He gave a tenpiastre note to the youthful interpreter, refused for a second time to buy the live squid, and escaped after an exchange of smiles, shrugs and vague handshakes. Behind him the puzzled Arabs still continued the argument amongst themselves, apparently undecided as to whether they had properly understood him.

"Well," Veronica said when they had retreated to a safe distance. "That seems to knock one wild idea smartly on its crazy little sun-touched head."

Roger grimaced wryly, making the funny face that always lightened their serious moments.

"It does rather. Even if we got far enough out to spot a passing ship we wouldn't be able to pretend we were in trouble with an Arab crew aboard. The only thing we could do now would be to steal a boat at night, but that would really be burning our boats behind us. We wouldn't be able to come back to Quseir, and if we didn't get picked up then we'd be finished. And I'm not quite that crazy."

"I'm glad to hear it." Veronica applauded.

Roger grinned. "We'll just have to fall back on to plan one. Wait until Kurt and Co. take us back to Quena, and then take a train to Alexandria. Meantime we'll just have to relax."

"Mmmm, suits me," she said, slipping her arm around him. "I keep trying to remember that I'm still supposed to be on my honeymoon."

★ ★ ★

Having resigned themselves to a period of inactivity they again spent the afternoon on the beach in the company of the three young Germans. They swam in the Red Sea, which was not really red but a dazzling, deep and vivid blue, and alternately roasted on the white,

228

eye-aching sand. They rubbed themselves liberally with suntan lotions, ate slices of ripe, juicy melon, and generally tried to forget everything but their immediate surroundings.

Late in the afternoon Kurt announced that he, Ernst and Walter intended to take a closer look at the old Napoleonic fort, but Roger professed himself too drowsy to move. The blond German smiled knowingly, and glanced at Veronica who looked more than inviting in an emerald green swimsuit. They had told him that they were only just married, and so he tactfully declined to press them. Instead the three Germans waved a casual goodbye as they set off across the sand.

When they had gone Veronica stirred and rested her head contentedly against Roger's shoulder. His arm encircled her and they lay under a large sunshade provided by the hotel and watched a dhow in full sail heading out to sea. They talked idly, kissed a little, and made plans for when they ultimately reached Alexandria. They wondered whether the search for them was still in full swing in Cairo, and then, to push away the last foreboding thought, they kissed some more.

They ran down to the sea for a final bathe as the sun set behind Quseir, and threw themselves into the darkening silver waves. They swam vigorously for half an hour and it was dusk as they walked back up the beach to dress. Roger stuffed their towels into the straw beach-bag they had bought the previous afternoon when they had gone shopping for their new swimsuits, and arm in arm they strolled back towards the hotel.

They were half way there when they encountered Inspector Kamal Hassain and two police sergeants walking calmly to meet them.

14

Battle Royal

The meeting was so completely unexpected that Roger could only stop dead and stare. Veronica was rendered equally incapable and uttered a little gasp of alarm as her body stiffened against his encircling arm. For a second they stood perfectly still, and by then it was too late to turn and run. One of the sergeants had automatically slipped the strap of his machine pistol from his shoulder and was holding the weapon across his body on a level with his hips. The gun's muzzle was not pointing at them directly, but the sergeant's eyes were fixed upon Roger's and that was warning enough.

Kamal Hassain smiled. The young Inspector still looked near-immaculate in his white uniform but there were tired shadows around his deep-set eyes. His dark jaw was still slightly swollen where

Roger had hit him, and he touched the spot gently with remembering fingers as he said.

"Good evening, Mr Stewart — and, of course, to your delightful young wife also. The two of you have led me quite a merry chase, but I think that now the fun and games are over. It would have been much better if you had simply accepted your fate in Cairo."

Roger still stood without moving. His left arm had tightened around Veronica's shoulders as she pressed against him, and the knuckles of his right hand had clenched white and helpless around the handle of the beach bag. The two sergeants had now moved methodically behind him and he knew that resistance was futile. He faced Hassain and said bitterly.

"How did you find us?"

"Quite simply, really," the inspector answered. "The boatman whom you bribed to take you down the Nile to Beni Suef was a loyal Egyptian, and he reported the matter quite naturally to the police. The report was passed on to me in Cairo and I drove down to Beni Suef to question the man. I showed him some enlargements I had had made from your passport photographs and the old man identified them immediately. After that it was routine, tiresome and time-consuming as always but it produced results. I placed a watch on the railway station and the roads, and of course I checked all the hotels and restaurants where you might have tried to eat. I finally found the hotel where you did purchase a meal, and the waiter remembered that you left with three German tourists. A shoe-cleaning boy who operates just outside the hotel was able to tell us that all five of you left in a Minibus and that you drove towards the south end of town. I notified all police stations along the Upper Nile and learned that although the Minibus had been seen as far south as Quena it had not appeared in Luxor. I could only deduce from that that you had turned off here to Quseir, and a telephone call proved me right. Consequently I came at once."

Roger listened with a sinking heart, and

again felt horribly out of his depth as he realized how easily they had been traced. It seemed pointless to say anything in return, but then he realized that there was one point that he was obliged to make. He drew a slow breath and said quietly.

"As you say, Inspector, the fun and games are over. But there is just one thing that I ought to make clear. The three German boys who gave us a lift had no idea that we were in trouble. We didn't tell them anything. We just allowed them to think that we were ordinary tourists."

Hassain shrugged. "They are unimportant. What matters is that roll of film you so unwisely accepted from the dancer-spy. We will return now to your hotel to retrieve it, and then we will all return once more to Cairo." He paused before adding. "And please do not make any further rash mistakes, Mr Stewart. I can assure you that Sergeants Kalman and Saardi are much more efficient than the two bungling fools who allowed you to escape from the Hotel Saladin the last time that we met."

Roger nodded slowly, for he had already appreciated that the two sergeants were a much different proposition to the two slovenly constables who had been the Inspector's previous companions. Kalman, the man who had already unslung his machine pistol, had an alert, toughened appearance, and for an Egyptian he was of unusually solid build. His companion Saardi was almost as big, but more Nubian in his features. They gave the impression of having been hand-picked for reliability, and made Roger realize even more how important the roll of film must be. It also made him realize how mightily he and Veronica had the odds stacked against them.

"Come," the Inspector insisted, a little more abruptly. "We will search your hotel room now."

Roger could not hesitate any longer and reluctantly he moved. He relaxed his grip on Veronica and took her arm instead and she walked dully at his side. He glanced at Hassain and said a little bitterly.

"You mean that you haven't searched the room yet? You must be slipping."

The Inspector smiled, for he could afford to smile at sour remarks. He said pleasantly.

"We have only just arrived here in Quseir, so we have not had time to visit your hotel. We went first to the police station here, and one of their constables mentioned that he had seen you lying on the beach. So, we decided to pick you up first."

Roger clamped his mouth shut against any answer, for he could feel a rising urge to spoil the Inspector's smug smile with another crack from his fist. Hassain noted the anger in his set face and simply smiled more broadly, but he allowed the silence to continue as they walked back to the hotel.

It was dark now but for the lights from the houses and shops that they passed, and above the stars were beginning to penetrate the blackness of the night sky. It was still very hot and the streets were lively. Radios blared shrill eastern music from dark rooms and children played in the gutters. A donkey plodded past, its back sagging beneath heavy straw panniers. Arab and Nubian faces stared with sharp curiosity, and then abruptly they were back at the hotel.

Kamal Hassain led the way inside. Roger followed him resignedly, still holding on to Veronica and their beach bag, while the two sergeants capably brought up the rear. The space behind the reception desk in the foyer was empty and Hassain rapped smartly on the desk-top with his knuckles. The bossy desk clerk failed to appear, and after a moment the Inspector scowled and then rapped again.

"It doesn't matter," Roger said wearily. "Our room is on the second floor. I'll show you."

Hassain looked at him and smiled. "Thank you, Mr Stewart, you are acting sensibly at last. What a pity that you could not have started our acquaintanceship in such a manner."

Roger said nothing, not trusting himself to speak, and simply indicated the stairs. Hassain led the way upwards and they followed slowly. On the second floor Roger pointed out the door of their bedroom, and they walked silently down the corridor.

Hassain stopped. "Is it locked?" he asked.

Roger shook his head, and with that Hassain turned and opened the door. He pushed it inwards and interrupted Shabetai and his two helpers in the middle of searching the room.

Unknown to Hassain, Shabetai had been close behind him all the way down the Nile. The report from Beni Suef had reached the Israeli almost as swiftly as it had reached the Inspector himself, and from then on the treacherous Sergeant Barrani had kept Shabetai fully informed.

The Israeli had left immediately for Beni Suef with Zadek and Ayoub, while the proprietor of the café where they had hidden near the Khan-El-Khalili had undertaken to note down any further messages from Barrani. On arrival at Beni Suef Shabetai had telephoned the café for Barrani's latest report, and learned that Hassain had continued down the Nile in search of the Volkswagen Minibus. From there keeping just one step behind the Inspector had proved simple, for Hassain had conscientiously reported every foot of his progress back to his headquarters in Cairo, and each report had passed through the chain of Barrani, the café near the Khan-El-Khalili, and finally to Shabetai. The informer had performed his task well, and when Kamal Hassain entered Quseir, Shabetai, by means of hard reckless driving across the last stretch of the desert road, was only minutes behind him.

The Israeli had recognized the Cairo police car standing outside the local police station, and had guessed that Hassain had stopped to consult his colleagues on the spot. He had realized that the Inspector's delay would give him a few valuable minutes, and fortunately there were few places in Quseir where the Stewarts and their new friends might be staying. Shabetai had driven straight to the most likely hotel, and breathed a sigh of relief when he saw the Volkswagen Minibus parked outside.

Swiftly he had led Zadek and Ayoub into the hotel. There had been no time to waste, and they had simply jammed a gun into the startled desk clerk and forced him to lead them upstairs to the room occupied by the English couple. Hastily they had commenced their search for the vital film, but their movements froze when they heard the voice of Kamal Hassain enquiring whether or not the door was locked from the corridor outside. Then, before they could even attempt to hide, the door had been thrust open and the white-uniformed figure of the Inspector appeared in the doorway.

★ ★ ★

Roger was only just behind Hassain, and over the Inspector's shoulder he saw the scene of wild disorder that had overtaken the room. The three intruders he recognized instantly as the three men who had attacked himself and Veronica at Karnak. The slim Israeli with the wavy-permed hair and steel spectacles was standing over the opened drawers of the dressing table. The nearer of his Arab companions had twisted guiltily away from the open wardrobe, and the second Arab stood against the far wall, holding the frightened youth from the reception desk with an automatic pressed against his cheek.

For an instant the tableau was rigid, and then everyone seemed to shout and move at once. Hassain and Shabetai uttered simultaneous cries of warning, and Ayoub frantically thrust the whimpering desk clerk away from him and raised his gun. Hassain sprang forward, and then ducked swiftly to one side in the room, his hand clawing at the flap of the buttoned revolver holster at his hip. Roger was already dropping flat and dragging Veronica with him to the floor. The reeling desk clerk stumbled in the same second and Ayoub fired over the youth's falling body.

The alert Sergeant Kalman had already stepped into the doorway, his ugly machine pistol levelled from his hip. His very alertness cost him his life as Ayoub's spitting bullet hit him below the chin and the hideous clatter of the machine pistol sprayed bullets at the ceiling as he fell backwards.

The next few minutes were bloody confusion as battle royal erupted in the cramped bedroom. Kamal Hassain failed to free his revolver before Shabetai had drawn his automatic, and in desperation the young Inspector hurled himself bodily at the Israeli. They collided in a struggling heap on the carpet and for a moment were too closely entangled for any of their subordinates to interfere. There was a sharp *Sput*! as Shabetai's silenced gun went off, and an agonized screech from the luckless desk clerk testified that the bullet had struck flesh.

The frantic Ayoub rushed for the door in the same moment, attempting to scramble over the cowering forms of Roger and Veronica, and the dead body of Kalman who had sprawled almost on top of them. He was almost there when he realized that Hassain had brought more than one companion, for Sergeant Saardi had quickly stepped to one side when the shooting had started. Now Saardi had unslung his own machine pistol and he stepped back into the doorway to bar the way. He stood with his feet astraddle the head and shoulders of the dead Kalman, and his dark, Nubian face bulged hotly with fury. Ayoub fired his automatic, but Saardi was a fraction faster. Ayoub's one small calibre bullet pinged off the wall, while the big Sergeant emptied half a magazine from his machine pistol into the Arab's body.

But there was still Zadek. Fortunately for him the angle of the door-post had shut him from Saardi's range of vision while the Sergeant had been still in the corridor. Like Ayoub he had believed the way of escape to be clear when Kalman had fallen and he too had rushed for the exit. He had stopped as the second Sergeant appeared to shoot his colleague down, and then he had realized that his only chance was to keep going. There was no time to fumble in his robes for his own gun, and so he simply hurled himself barehanded at Saardi before the other could switch the aim of his machine pistol.

As the two men collided above him, and then fell fighting inside the room, Roger risked lifting his head for the first time. He saw that both Kalman and Ayoub had died in the hideous exchange of gunfire, and that the four survivors were fighting two separate battles on the floor of the bedroom. The Egyptian desk clerk was huddled in a corner, crying and holding a bleeding shoulder.

Quickly Roger scrambled to his feet and helped Veronica up beside him. The shambles and the sight of blood and death had given him his first taste of deep, panic-stricken fear, and there was only one thought left in his mind.

"Ronnie," he urged frantically. "Come on, let's get out of here!"

He dragged her away from the doorway and she almost fell again as he struggled to hold her up. The sight of Kalman lying with the blood welling up from the ragged hole beneath his chin had shattered her nerves and it was with difficulty that she pulled herself together. They stumbled, white-faced, down the stairs, and then fled out of the hotel into the night.

★ ★ ★

Back in the wreckage of the bedroom the battle still raged. Theoretically the two Egyptian policemen should have won easily, for they had the advantages of weight and strength. However, in each case their opponents were inflamed to the point of madness; Shabetai by his own driving, inner fanaticism, and Zadek by the fact that Ayoub had been not only his friend but also his lover. For several minutes they fought furiously before weight finally prevailed. Saardi managed to throw off the lighter Zadek, and a moment later he regained his fallen machine pistol. He shouted a command, crouching on one knee, and Zadek slowly backed away.

Panting hard the Sergeant stood up. Hassain and Shabetai rolled apart and the Inspector quickly freed his revolver. Shabetai had already been forced to drop his automatic and Hassain kicked it beneath the bed as he too got shakily to his feet.

"Thank you, Sergeant," he approved weakly.

He glared at the Israeli and the surviving Arab, and without waiting for orders they both placed their hands nervously upon their heads. He glanced round farther and his smooth young face grew harder as he saw that Kalman was dead, then abruptly he realized that his two prisoners were missing. He swore, rapped instructions to Saardi, and then sprinted in pursuit.

Behind him Saardi stood splay-legged, his finger itching on the trigger of the machine pistol. On the floor Shabetai was helpless without his spectacles which had broken in the fighting, and he sat in miserable silence. Zadek looked at the bloodied corpse of Ayoub and pitifully he began to cry.

★ ★ ★

In the streets outside Roger and Veronica were already running back towards the beach as hard as they could go. Roger gripped his wife's hand as he ran, and strangely his right hand still clung on fiercely to their straw beach bag. Had he thought about it he would doubtless have thrown it away in order to run more swiftly, but even though he held it so tightly it was completely forgotten. He was only aware of the dozens of dark, curious faces that followed their flight as they plunged through the streets, and he knew despairingly that as soon as any pursuit started up the majority of those staring faces would be only too willing to point out the way that they had gone.

He slowed his pace in order to be less noticeable, and pulled Veronica back beside him. She was breathing heavily, and for the moment was still too shocked by the bloodshed they had just witnessed to make any suggestions or decisions, and he knew that temporarily all the moves were up to him. He fought down some of his own panic and tried to think.

The only course that he could see was

to steal a car or some kind of vehicle, and then attempt to recross the desert road to the Nile. But there were no cars available. He thought of the Volkswagen Minibus in the hotel yard behind them, and although in his present plight he could have crushed down his conscience and taken it, he knew that it would be foolish to go back in that direction. Then a swell of loud, excited voices from the street they had just left told him exactly how foolish, and he realized that the pursuit had already started.

He swore, for he had hoped for more time while Hassain and his Sergeant were subduing the Israelies, and once more he broke into a run. The sounds behind were too close for any delay, and he realized bitterly that as the only two Europeans in the streets he and Veronica were wholly conspicuous anyway.

For a few more moments they slipped and stumbled over the rough road surface, but then Veronica recovered herself a little and began to run more strongly. Then abruptly they were out on the darkened beach again, and began to run across the sand. They were alone now, with no jostling crowds on either side to point the way to whoever followed, and Roger began to revive his hopes. Ahead lay the black calmness of the sea, transparent along its rippling edge and placid in the starlight. To their left lay the dark, ghostly shapes of some boats drawn up upon the sand and it was towards these that Roger headed, hoping to regain his breath in their shadow. Then a voice shouted angrily from behind.

He twisted clumsily, catching at Veronica as the sudden halt almost caused her to fall, and stared back at the lone man sprinting across the beach towards them. The white uniform showed up clearly in the night and his hopes crashed as he recognized Kamal Hassain. He hesitated on the point of surrender and then Hassain stretched out an arm towards him and the crack of his heavy police revolver rang above the silent sands.

The bullet passed close and was definitely no mere warning. Roger's heart did a somersault and the fleeting thought of surrender flashed away as he grabbed at Veronica's arm and continued their hectic flight.

Another bullet whined above their heads but Roger knew that it would be no easy task for one running man to hit another and so he kept going. A moment later he reached the group of stranded fishing boats and ducked behind the nearest hull. They dodged among the leaning hulks and then he pushed Veronica down into the dark patch of shadow by the keel of a large dhow.

"Stay there," he gasped. "Stay there and don't move!"

"But, Roger, what — ?"

"Hassain was shooting to kill," he explained. "He must have decided that we really are in with that other bunch, and now they've murdered one of his Sergeants he's playing just as rough with us. I've got to get that gun away before I can talk sense to him."

"But, Roger — "

Her anguished cry trailed off into a tiny sob as she realized that he was not listening. Already he was slipping away through the miniature maze of hulls and she could only crouch lower into her patch of shadow and wait.

A moment later Kamal Hassain reached the cluster of hauled up boats, and for a moment he hesitated on the spot where he had last seen his quarry. As Roger had guessed he was furious, and determined that no pair of amateurs would make him look a fool for the second time. Also his nerves had been badly rasped by the abrupt death of his Sergeant, and his present mood was a policy of shoot first and put a finish to any further complications.

Cautiously, the Inspector moved among the boats. There was no sign of the two fugitives on the open sand beyond and so he guessed that they must be hiding somewhere close. He tried to distinguish their trail in the sand, but here it was too fine and powdery to leave any defined print. He breathed heavily as he moved among the ancient hulls, and his chest was rising and falling with almost painful regularity. The fact made him suddenly realize that the two he followed must

251

be equally as breathless, and with an effort he stopped breathing and listened carefully.

There was complete silence amongst the scattered hulls. Hassain could feel the pressure building up in his own chest but he held out against it — and then he was rewarded by the sound of a whispering intake of breath from beneath one of the boats. He moved towards it, drawing in his own breath and smiling, and firmly gripping his revolver. He made out the huddled shape in the dark patch by the keel of the large dhow, but before he could distinguish whether the shape was made up of one body or two there was a scratching sound behind him.

He twisted in the same moment that Roger launched himself bodily from the deck of the nearest boat and together they crashed down on to the sand. Hassain was underneath and both his revolver and his cap went rolling away as the breath was forced from his body. Roger made a scrambling effort to reach the gun, but somehow Hassain caught him by the hips and dug both thumbs viciously into his groin. Roger twisted away with a howl of agony and their wrestling movements took them away from the fallen revolver.

Veronica emerged from beneath the keel of the dhow and picked up the fallen weapon, but for the moment there was nothing that she could do with it. The two men were rolling and kicking so violently that even if she had tried to use it as a club she would have risked hitting Roger.

For several wild, savage moments they fought in the darkened arena between the boats. Then Roger's shoulders crashed against a rotting hull and in the same moment he managed to drive his knee into the pit of Hassain's stomach. They separated as Roger struggled up, and Veronica made an attempt to caution the Inspector with his own gun. Hassain replied by hurling sand in her face and charging Roger once more as she stumbled away.

With an effort Roger retained his balance, despite Hassain having both arms wrapped around his hips. They staggered for a moment, and then Hassain reached his feet. Roger pushed him away and swung a punch that missed, and Hassain countered with a smashing chopping blow to the throat. Fortunately the blow missed its intended target and struck high, but even so it rocked Roger's head and slammed his back against the stern of the dhow. Hassain came in again and desperately Roger lashed out with a terrific straight right. The punch was a beauty that took Hassain squarely on the point of the chin. The young Inspector seemed to arch almost gracefully backwards, his arms flailing slowly, and there was a strange, mushy crunching noise as he fell.

Roger stood panting as Veronica moved to help him, and for a moment he was incapable of either thought or movement. He stood with his eyes shut for a few seconds, and when he opened them his vision was still a little hazy. He looked down at Hassain, and quite suddenly he realized that the young Inspector was much too still. There was no slight chest movement as there would have been with an unconscious man, and instead he was completely motionless. Roger felt suddenly afraid, and starkly, vividly he recalled the mushy crunch as Hassain had fallen.

He moved closer, and he saw the upthrust point of a boat's anchor jutting from the sand close by Hassain's head. And then he saw the dark stain on the sand itself where the back of the Inspector's skull had been crushed inwards.

15

Adrift

There was an utter stillness now about the night. The long, slanting masts of the leaning boats made a ghostly pattern against the stars, like the bare stems of wilted flowers from a funerary bouquet. They made a graveyard of dead ships from the abandoned circle on the sand. The very silence was oppressive and both Roger and Veronica stood as though mesmerized. Then the sound of their own tensed breathing broke the spell, and Veronica took a tentative step towards the outstretched body of Kamal Hassain. Roger caught her shoulder sharply and drew her back. She looked at him with horror-struck eyes, and he pushed her gently to one side before he moved to examine the Inspector.

There was no hope in his heart, and immediately he wished that he had not knelt to take that closer look. Hassain's head had hit squarely upon the rusting point of the blunted anchor, and there was no doubt that he had been killed instantly. Roger turned away feeling queasy in the pit of his stomach.

Veronica said weakly. "Is he dead?"

Roger nodded. "His head caved in like an eggshell." He found Hassain's cap and with fumbling fingers placed it over the dead man's face. He stood up and said bitterly.

"What a filthy thing to happen. I only wanted to get that gun away from him long enough to explain that we didn't know anything about those three men at the hotel. I'm sure he believed that we led him into a trap because of the way he started shooting at us." He stared at the half-buried anchor and finished shakily. "The poor sod — he was only doing his job after all."

Veronica gripped his arm nervously.

"But what about us, Roger? Even though it was an accident he still died because you were fighting him. They'll charge you with murder."

The word struck a chill through his bowels, but he knew that she was right. They were no longer running from a prison sentence but for their very lives. Strangely enough, the knowledge steadied him, for it impressed upon him the need to keep his head and think clearly. He looked back towards Quseir and saw that as yet there were no further signs of pursuit, and was thankful for the fact that Hassain had been alone.

He said grimly. "That second Sergeant — Saardi — Hassain must have left him to watch over the Israelies, or whatever was left of them, but even so we can't have much time. All that gunfire must have attracted the local police, and the moment some of them reach the hotel Saardi will be pelting after Hassain and us. We've got to get moving."

Veronica nodded, and automatically she picked up their beach bag which Roger had dropped beside her before tackling the Inspector, and she dropped the heavy police revolver that she was holding inside.

"Where to?" she asked.

"Back to the hotel. We'll try a roundabout route and try and pinch the Minibus. It's a lousy way to repay Kurt and the boys after the way they've befriended us, but to them it will only mean an inconvenience whereas now our lives are at stake. In the circumstances I think they'd understand."

He started to drag her away from the cluster of boats, but she pulled back.

"No, Roger," she said desperately. "It's no good. The local police will be swarming round that hotel for hours yet. We'd never be able to steal the Minibus. And Quseir's not like Cairo, it's only a small town and we're the only white couple here. As soon as we show our faces there'll be a hue and cry."

"We've got to try," he said helplessly. "At least we've got to try."

"But not that way," she insisted. "We'll be better off stealing a boat. We can follow your original plan and escape out to sea."

He stared at her, and then said slowly. "Ronnie, the Red Sea is the hottest sea on the face of the earth. My plan was simply to sail out daily, and if nothing happened to return every night — not to cast off with no food or water and risk all or nothing on our chances of being picked up. We could die out there."

She nodded wretchedly, but then her chin lifted and she gazed up into his face. "I can see that, darling, but it's our only chance of getting out of Egypt now. Even if you did manage to steal the Minibus there is still only the one road out of Quseir. It's a five-hour journey across the desert and that's plenty of time for a telephone call to reach Quena and have us stopped."

There were tears in her eyes as she finished earnestly.

"Roger, we must escape now. If we stay we're sure to be caught — and I'd rather die with you in the middle of the Red Sea, rather than go into an Egyptian prison knowing that you were to be hanged for killing the Inspector."

Roger wavered, and then slowly he realized that she was right. Their only choice lay in attempting to steal one of the fishing boats, or resigning themselves to Egyptian justice. In regard to the latter he reminded himself of the *Hate Britain* campaign that Egypt's Colonel Nasser had long been fermenting in Aden and the Yemen, and he guessed that justice for an Englishman would hold little mercy. Also there was the fact that the brother of the man he had accidentally killed was certain to be the man in charge of his arrest and trial, and he knew that Major Faizal Hassain would demand the ultimate penalty.

Veronica was still awaiting his reply, and he nodded slowly.

"All right. Ronnie, it's all or nothing. We'll make our break out to sea."

She looked relieved, but there was no time now for any further discussion. The few whispered moments they had already wasted could even now prove fatal, and so they hurried away from the cluster of beached hulls that hid the still body of the unfortunate Inspector. They ran down to the sea's edge, and then turned to run along the silvered shallows, heading for the harbour and the boats they had examined earlier that morning.

Across the beach there was still no sound of any further pursuit from the streets of Quseir, and they could only assume that Sergeant Saardi and the local police forces were still being delayed by the Israelies. Roger prayed that the situation would remain so, and despite the fact that both he and Veronica were almost at their last gasp he kept running at full speed. The gentle wavelets splashed around their ankles, but the sand here was firm and flat and did not cause them any falls or stumbles.

They reached a group of three seaworthy boats drawn up just above the level of the sea, and came to a panting, slithering halt. Their arrival caused no reaction from the silent craft and Roger realized that their luck was in and that all three boats were deserted. He glanced around swiftly to ensure that their dash through the shallows had not been noticed, and then turned to examine the boats more closely.

All three were built on the inevitable lines of the Arab dhow, but the second one in the line was again fitted with a small auxiliary engine. The boat was about twenty feet long, and although Roger had hoped to find something smaller he knew that he did not have time to be choosy. He took their beach bag from Veronica and tossed it aboard, and together they strained to ease the dhow out into deep water.

It took them five minutes of back-breaking struggle to move the clumsy craft into the shallows, but once she became more buoyant the task was easier. A final thrust from Roger caused the hull to straighten, the high mast becoming more upright, and then he helped the near-exhausted Veronica to climb aboard. He returned to the stern of the dhow and pushed her slowly out to sea until the low waves were swirling around his chest, and then he hauled himself up beside his wife. Veronica helped him to climb on to the deck, and with salt water dripping from his shirt and jeans he stumbled over to the small, alarmingly ancient-looking engine.

The sight of the engine filled him with despair, but despite its age and the vast quantities of rust on some of its outer components it finally worked. The vital parts seemed to have been well cared for, and after a few minutes of feverish false starts the motor spluttered into healthy life. Roger stared at it unbelievingly for a second, and then he grabbed quickly for the tiller, steering directly out to sea and praying that they would be well out of sight before any pursuit could catch them up.

Veronica touched his arm as they chugged slowly out towards the invisible horizon, and glancing back he realized that at last there were signs of activity on the beach they had left. The starlight was not bright enough for them to see what was happening, but shouts and movements told them that Saardi had finally arrived with reinforcements and was searching for his Inspector. Roger felt his heart thumping and gingerly shut down their engine so that they made only a soft murmur of noise as they slowly lengthened the distance between the dhow and the shore. So far they had escaped unseen, and as long as the local fishermen did not immediately realize that one of their boats was missing they still had a slim chance.

* * *

By dawn they were adrift far out in the Red Sea. Roger had steered a straight course directly away from Quseir throughout the night until their obsolete but game little engine had given a final splutter and died from lack of petrol. There were no spare cans on board and so they were at the mercy of winds and tide. The great furled sail lashed to the mast was useless to them, for Roger had no knowledge of sailing and he doubted whether he could have hoisted the sail even with Veronica's help. In any case, he reckoned that they were far enough out from the coast to be in the wide shipping lanes that flowed down from Suez, and so they could only hope for the best.

They were both dozing when the stars paled into the morning light, and the sun peeped its one crimson eye over the eastern rim of the horizon. It was a vivid sunrise, as though the one eye was weeping tears of blood over sky and sea. Roger stirred with his back pressed against the tiller, and glanced down at Veronica who lay at right angles to him across the deck, her cheek pillowed against his thigh. For a while he simply watched the sun rising out of the sea, but then a slight bout of cramp made him move his leg and Veronica awoke.

She sat up uncertainly, and gazed at the vast, empty expanse of calm sea that surrounded their small dhow, glancing only briefly at the pageant of glowing colour in the eastern sky. Only the emptiness impressed her, and she asked nervously.

"Where are we?"

"About as far out as we can get." Roger helped her to sit upright and added with forced confidence. "All we have to do now is to wait for a ship to come past and wave it down."

Veronica turned her head to look behind them.

"Do you think Saardi will try to follow

us? This boat must have been missed by now."

Roger shrugged. "He might, but I don't think that we need to worry about that angle. We saw no fast motorboats of any kind at Quseir which they might use to make an effective search, so if he and the local police do try to follow they'll be reduced to a fishing boat the same as us. Besides, they have no way of knowing the exact direction of our escape, and most probably they'll waste time searching along the coast first. Their chances of finding our little dhow in all this sea are pretty remote."

"And our chances of being picked up?"

Roger realized that his last comment had been hardly tactful, but he tried to make amends.

"Stop worrying," he ordered. "They're looking for one particular fishing boat, while we can flag down any south-bound ship we happen to see. Even without water we can last for two or three days, and we're sure to spot a ship before then."

Veronica smiled faintly. "I won't worry," she promised. "At least we've escaped from Egypt, and we're still alive."

"That's my girl!" He kissed her cheek, and then added somewhat dubiously. "I can't help wishing that we had managed to retain the film though. That was the cause of all our troubles and it would have been a triumph to hand it over to the British authorities in Aden. Now we'll never know what it was all about."

Veronica raised her eyebrows. "But, Roger, we have got the film. At least I think so. I put it in the beach bag."

"You did what?"

"The beach bag," she repeated. "I didn't trust that bossy little clerk at the hotel so I thought it best to keep the film with us. It's at the bottom of the bag beneath our towels and swimsuits." She paused, and finished blankly. "I thought you knew. I thought that was why you hung on to the bag last night."

"Well, I'll be damned," Roger said. He reached for the straw bag that lay upon the deck a yard away and checked that the roll of film really was there. He held it up and grinned.

"Ronnie, you're a treasure. With a bit of luck we will know what it was all about after all."

Veronica made a face which signified how unimportant she considered that aspect of the situation, and then asked.

"Shouldn't we start keeping watch, or something?"

"It might be advisable," Roger admitted.

He got to his feet and painstakingly searched the far encircling line of the horizon. There was no sail, no puff of smoke, and no sign of any living thing. Veronica stood up beside him and they exchanged doubtful looks.

"It's early yet," Roger said hopefully. "Even in London you usually have to wait half an hour for a bus, so we can't really expect a ship to pop up here the very first time we take a squint at the skyline." He gripped her arm and finished. "Come on, we'll explore our luxury pleasure yacht while we wait."

Exploring the dhow took very little time, for there was nothing there to explore. There was a hold, or at least an open hatch that gave entry to the space between the deckboards and the boat's hull, but there was nothing inside except a strong smell of dead fish and some scraps of rotting net. They peered inside, wrinkled their noses, and then walked to the bows of the boat and back again. There was nothing that they could put to the slightest use and their explorations were complete.

They stood together by the mast and again they scanned the horizon. Again it was empty, and the only change in their surroundings was that the sun was steadily gaining altitude to the east. Already the heat was a real threat.

They maintained their watch until the sun was roasting them cruelly from above, and then they attempted to keep cool by taking turns to slip over the side into the sea. The dhow was all but becalmed so there was no danger of either of them being swept away. The short swims helped to revive their spirits for the next two hours, until abruptly their pleasures were interrupted by a new danger that both of them had forgotten. Veronica was splashing happily a few yards away from the dhow, while Roger stood against the mast, his head protected from sunstroke by a towel as he wearily surveyed the skyline. He tired of his vigil and his attention wandered for a moment, and it was then that he saw the sharp triangular fin moving dreamily through the water only thirty yards away.

He gave a frantic yell of warning and hurriedly dived for their beach bag and Kamal Hassain's gun. Veronica swam hastily towards him and he was trembling as he helped her aboard. The cruising shark was not apparently hungry, for it did not come close enough to warrant a shot from the big police revolver, but it effectively terminated any further swimming.

It was after that that the terrible, scorching heat really began to tell on them. Fortunately their beach bag still contained suntan lotions and dark glasses, and their towels made passable turbans, but there was a vast difference between lazing on the beach beneath the hotel sunshade and being grilled on the white-hot deckboards of the dhow with no escape. Their strength drained, and they began to suffer the first craving pangs of thirst.

As the afternoon wore on they sat listlessly on the deck of the dhow, standing up only at intervals to make their fruitless search of the horizon. They talked to keep their spirits up, but they no longer talked of Egypt or Aden, of the mysterious roll of film or the ship which they hoped would ultimately pick them up. Instead they talked quietly of home; of London and England; of their respective families and work. The staid, hushed atmosphere of the distant architect's office with its grey wallpaper and brown carpets, and the drizzle falling outside its windows, all seemed very far removed in both miles and time.

Veronica said softly. "It all seems so very long ago now, and yet at the same time it's as clear as yesterday. All those lovely plans we made during our coffee breaks, and all those brochures about the pyramids that I kept hidden under my typewriter with the guest list for our wedding."

Roger smiled. "I re-wrote that guest list five times. Once on the back of a drawing for part of the new grammar school which they threw out and then decided they wanted back again. They were narked about that."

"They weren't too bad," she said. "It was a good firm."

"Perhaps you're right. They were good to us. And after all this I think I'll be glad to get back to my own drawing board. I might even redesign that dull old grammar school with Karnak-styled columns." He smiled at her. "How about you? Will you enjoy being a virgin secretary once more?"

Faintly she returned his smile. "You should know that I can never go back to being a virgin anything any more. But I would like to go back — just until we start a family. It was fun sometimes. The other girls were nice and friendly . . . "

And so they talked on, about the office, about mutual friends, about shows they had seen and books they had read; in fact about anything but the sweltering heat and their parched throats. Anything but the glaring sun and the empty sea. Anything at all that could provide a verbal insulation from the harsh nightmare around them.

At last the long tortuous hours of daylight passed, and they watched the dying sun sink in a blaze of final glory to the west. By now their thirst was an agony of dry throats and peeling lips, and they welcomed the darkness as a blessing. Their voices were little more than a husky croak, and they wearily decided to sleep in turns so that one of them would always be on the lookout for a passing ship. To spot them at night a ship would have to pass almost on top of them, but they dared not take the chance of missing anything that might come along. Veronica stretched out wearily to sleep and Roger took the first watch.

He stood by the mast, and inside he was a very worried man. The effects of the last few hours had been much more drastic than he had expected for the first day, and he had to face the fact that neither of them could last as long without water as he had previously hoped. Also he was forced to realize that even here in the Red Sea shipping was not as plentiful as he had optimistically believed. He had expected to see glimpses of ships on the horizon even if they had not come near enough to see him, but throughout the day there had not been as much as a single puff of smoke.

He noticed shortly after that that the dhow was moving, caught in some slow tide or current, but it hardly seemed important. The starlight made a fairly clear night and he strained his eyes to find the lights of some passing vessel, but nothing broke the blackness of the horizon.

They both snatched brief spells of sleep at intervals through the night, but dawn found them both awake and huddled together to watch their second sunrise. This time they watched with the fascination of trapped rabbits, fixed by the rising head of some glaring red cobra, for now the sun was their prime enemy.

They bridged their eyes to scan the horizon but still to no avail. There was nothing there. The day grew hotter and the terrible sun rose higher in the scorching sky. They were already weak and the renewed agonies of thirst came much swifter. The Red Sea basked placidly in its reputation of being the hottest stretch of water on the face of the earth.

There was no conversation now, for their lips had cracked and their throats were too dehydrated to form the words. The insulating memories of home that had aided them yesterday could not relieve their ordeal today. They could only sit and wait, and stare at the empty sea with red and aching eyes.

And then they saw the ship.

She was a toy, a perfectly formed toy balanced on the rim of their world, her single smokestack puffing a fairytale streamer of white cloud into the searing blue sky. She was going north, back to Suez and Egypt, but anything was better now than a lingering death on the dhow and Roger hailed her as loudly as his moistureless throat would allow.

The distant toy sailed peacefully on its way.

Roger screamed hoarsely, tearing off his towel turban and waving it frantically above his head. Veronica followed his example and they both rushed to the stern of the dhow. They shouted until their voices were so weak that they could barely hear each other, and then Roger stumbled back to the centre of the dhow and clawed his way up the swaying mast. He got ten feet above the deck and waved his towel again.

The faraway ship merely grew smaller, its stern towards them now as it sank out of sight beyond the skyline. Soon it had vanished altogether.

Roger clung feebly to the mast, his eyes closed and the merciless sun pounding down on his now unprotected head. There were splinters in his hands and he was not sure of the best way of getting down. Then the noise of sobbing told him that Veronica had collapsed on the deck, and letting go his hold he dropped clumsily on his hands and knees beside her. He put his arm around her shuddering shoulders and gently drew her close, but there was nothing, absolutely nothing, that he could say.

16

The Secret of the Film

With an effort Roger propped his back against the dhow's mast, and managed to rearrange his towel over his head to protect himself from the full blast of the sun. He did the same for Veronica and cradled her in his arms, and after a while her sobbing ceased and she became still. She lifted her head and looked up at him slowly, and her hazel eyes were horribly rimmed with red. A dull strand of her chestnut hair clung limply to her forehead where the skin was already raw and starting to blister. Her haunted expression told him that he looked no better, and when she hoisted herself feebly in his arms he held her more tightly. There was no room for words, and in any case their frantic shouting had left them too husky to speak. Instead he lowered his mouth and touched her cracked lips with a gentle, totally arid kiss. Her eyes closed and she lay very still in his arms.

For a moment he thought she was dead, but strangely there was no remorse. Soon he would follow her and he was glad that she had not been the one to linger and die alone. Then he realized that there was still life in her body, and he laid his cheek against her own so that he could hear the soft, blessed whisper of her breathing.

He had no idea of how long he sat like that, holding Veronica with his back to the mast and the full sun blazing down from directly above. He simply sat, waiting for death, but from time to time he forced himself to raise his head and search the endless glaring emptiness of the sea.

Each time he raised his head despair crushed more heavily on the dimming embers of hope, and the periods of staring helplessly at the deck grew longer and longer. Until finally he looked up, and there, less than a mile away through the misty haze of his vision, was a mirage.

It was glittering and beautiful, the mirage of a great, white-hulled liner cruising sedately across the calm sea. He knew that it had to be a mirage, for it was so close, and it had not been there when he had looked a moment before.

He watched it carefully, and tried to count the tiny black pinpricks that were its portholes. He decided that he was going mad, but at least he would not go outwardly mad and dance about insanely over a mirage. Then he became aware of a strange fact, for the mirage had a wake that stretched back to the horizon. Surely a mirage would be localized, he thought dully, it wouldn't leave a trail.

Then the truth dawned as he suddenly realized that the sun had moved its position since he had last looked up a moment ago. That moment had been at least an hour and in his heat-exhausted condition he could no longer judge time. He shook Veronica and mercifully her eyes opened. She twisted her head and hope flickered in her face as he excitedly pointed out the ship.

Its appearance gave them new heart,

and it seemed almost too good to be true that it was heading south away from the Suez Canal. They struggled up and waved their towels, croaking hoarsely in an effort to attract the ship's attention.

The big luxury liner sailed on. They could see it clearly now, two large, slanting funnels, and a tiered superstructure like slabs of smooth iced wedding cake. Roger even convinced himself that the flag at her stern was the famed Red Duster of the British merchant fleet, and it seemed impossible that the men on her bridge could not in turn see the dhow. They waved frantically but the ship showed no signs of stopping, and at last he turned bitterly to Veronica.

"It's no good, darling," The croaked words were barely audible. "They can't hear us, and even if they can see us they must think that we're just a couple of Arab fishermen cheering them on their way."

She nodded wearily, and came to stand beside him. The ship was still in sight but was gradually showing them her stern, and they both succumbed to the hopelessness of defeat. And then suddenly Veronica stiffened.

"Roger," she blurted desperately. "What about the gun?"

He stared at her, and slowly remembered Kamal Hassain's heavy police revolver that reposed in the beach bag on the deck behind them. The memory spurred him into action and he quickly turned to empty the straw bag out on to the deck. He grabbed up the revolver and returned to Veronica in the stern of the dhow. She smiled faintly and put her arm round him, and then he pointed the revolver in the air and fired.

The sharp crack sounded clear through the still air, ringing out across the placid sea. Roger counted a careful twenty seconds and then fired again. After that they both continued their frantic waving.

At intervals he continued to fire off the revolver into the air, but after five shots it was empty. They could only maintain their waving then and hope, but after a few minutes they saw that the wake of the distant ship was making a slow curve. The liner was losing way and coming round.

For the next hour they watched as the mighty vessel manoeuvred round to pick them up, and finally she hove-to only a hundred yards away while one of her lifeboats was lowered. Her rails were now lined with hundreds of curious passengers, and they could see the name on her proud bows, the *Judith Rose*. From her masthead flew the white flag with the red rose emblem of the Rose Line Shipping Company. The lifeboat that was rowed out to meet them was commanded by the ship's Third Officer, and willing hands soon helped Roger and Veronica aboard. They left the dhow to drift and returned briskly to the *Judith Rose*, and once the boat had been hoisted back to its davits on the parent vessel's upper deck the two castaways were helped down into the ship's hospital. Neither of them were in any fit state to answer questions, and so they were spared any immediate need to explain themselves. The ship's doctor sparingly gave them water, and after he and his nurse had attended to the ravages of their ordeal they were allowed to sleep off its worst effects.

＊ ＊ ＊

When they were sufficiently recovered to talk they faced an uncomfortable interview with the ship's master, and Captain Hugh B. Maitland was as impressive in himself as the long string of knighthoods and decorations that followed his name. He was grey-haired, solid and authoritative, and not at all pleased with the interruption they had caused to the smooth running of his ship. He listened with growing disapproval to Roger's story of having run out of petrol on a fishing trip, and then demolished it by asking brusquely.

"If that's the truth then you're a pair of damned fools — but just as a matter of interest, tell me how you acquired that damned great gun you were blazing away with to attract our attention?"

Roger faltered awkwardly, and then decided that his attempts at subterfuge had already boomeranged upon him far too frequently. The Captain, despite his formidable frown, was still British, and so Roger launched into a frank account of their true story.

Maitland was still frowning when he had finished, but now it was a more thoughtful frown. He looked from one to the other and said severely.

"You're a bigger pair of fools than I realized. Getting yourselves into a mess with the Egyptian police was bad enough, but to deliberately push off into the Red Sea without a single mouthful of water was practically suicide. It may look small compared to the Atlantic or the Pacific, but there's still a hell of a lot of sea out there. You were very lucky indeed."

His expression caused Veronica to squirm a little on her chair, and even Roger was afraid that his face was going to flush with embarrassment. And then Maitland relaxed suddenly and gave a brief smile.

"Two very lucky fools," he repeated. "But I suppose one must not condemn the traditional bulldog spirit. If Britain had not always been liberally sprinkled with madmen with a flair for doing the wrong thing right and never having the sense to admit defeat, then we would have always remained an island and never an Empire. But now I think that you had best give this roll of mysterious film to me, and I'll have it locked in the Purser's safe to make sure that it doesn't cause any more trouble."

Roger nodded slowly, and handed over the small tin canister that held the roll of fim. The Captain looked at it dubiously and then placed it on the table beside him.

Roger said. "What happens now, sir? To the film — and us?"

"Well the *Judith Rose* is bound for Australia," Maitland said calmly. "But our next port of call will be Aden in two days time. That's where I shall hand the two of you and your film over to the British authorities — after that I can't say." He smiled suddenly. "You needn't be afraid that I'll turn round and take you back to Egypt if that's what worries you. Of course, I've had to inform the Egyptian authorities that I've picked you up, as well as radioing reports to Aden and my head office in London, but it's too costly for there to be any question of taking you back. No matter what you or the Egyptians may desire you will be put ashore at Aden."

Roger smiled and said. "That suits us perfectly."

★ ★ ★

Two days later, at three in the afternoon, the *Judith Rose* sighted the harsh peninsula of volcanic rock that sprawled in twin, sentinel peaks around the Bay of Aden. She dropped her anchor at Steamer Point at the head of the low, sandy isthmus on the west side of the bay, and lay there with her white decks gleaming in the brilliant sunshine. Aden itself was a white-bleached outpost on a barren corner of the vast, desert land-mass of Arabia, a strategic refuelling point and nothing else.

The liner was not due to continue her voyage to Australia until the following morning, but after an hour a British Police Inspector arrived to take Roger and Veronica ashore. They were handed

288

over in the Captain's cabin, and Maitland had softened enough to wish them luck.

They were whisked away from Steamer Point in a closed police car, and taken to a police station in the main part of the town. The film was rushed away for immediate development, and meanwhile they were subjected to a lengthy cross-examination from the young Inspector whose name was Bartlett.

Despite its length the interrogation was on a friendly basis, and Roger kept nothing back. Bartlett frowned grimly when they recounted how Kamal Hassain had met his death, but although he obviously had a strong sympathy for a man who had only been doing the same job as he was doing himself he accepted that it had been an accident. He asked innumerable questions, taking them over the same ground several times, but eventually he had some long statements typed out which they read and signed. After that they were given a respite and a meal.

There was a long wait, and it was late evening before they were sent for again.

This time they were driven to another building where Bartlett took them inside and into another small office. Here he left them to face yet another interrogation from a middle-aged, sandy-haired man behind a cluttered desk.

The man welcomed them with a smile, standing up and offering Roger his hand. He had a firm, brief grip, and he wore civilian clothes with an air of quiet efficiency.

"Let me introduce myself," he said. "My name is Jackson. My rank and position are not important, but that roll of film which you managed to bring out of Egypt lies more within the field of my own department than with the civilian police. That's why Inspector Bartlett has handed you over to me."

He indicated two comfortable chairs and invited them to sit, and then he moved his own chair round to the front of the desk and relaxed informally in front of them.

"I know you've already been through everything with Inspector Bartlett," he went on. "And I've read through both your statements. But if you don't mind I would like to hear it all again, just in case I can pick up a few more grains of information — something you might not have thought worth while and the Inspector might have missed."

Somewhat wearily Roger went through the whole thing once again. Jackson listened with one hand resting on his knee, and the other occasionally tugging at his jaw. When Roger hesitated he offered cigarettes or cups of tea, or else glanced at Veronica to invite her to help him out. The session proved to be the smoothest yet, and at the end of it Jackson asked a wide range of penetrating questions. He seemed satisfied at last and said.

"Well, Mr Stewart, I think we've covered everything, at least well enough to set the records straight. The next thing — and no doubt the most important thing from your point of view — is what are we going to do with you?"

Roger shrugged his shoulders helplessly, and after a moment Veronica asked.

"Will the Egyptians be able to extradite

us — or anything like that?"

"Well, so far they haven't made any such request and as they've had plenty of time to do so, I think that we can assume that they'd rather not publicize the affair. Even so we won't take the risk of sending you home on a ship that has to pass through Suez where you might be taken off. I don't suppose that you have much money so the best thing is to wait until there are a couple of seats on one of our regular R.A.F. flights and then have you flown straight home. I think that I can arrange that." He smiled and finished. "I think that the worst you'll probably have to face now is a very nasty letter from the Foreign Office, demanding to know exactly how you came to lose your passports."

Roger exchanged relieved smiles with Veronica, and then after a moment's hesitation he asked.

"What about the film, sir? Can we know what it was all about?"

Jackson frowned dubiously and tugged at his jaw. Then he studied them with shrewd blue eyes and finally said.

"After all you've been through I suppose you are entitled to know. I had that film developed as soon as it was brought to me and all thirty-six frames came out. One or two of them were a little blurred by too much light, but our experts have been able to make them all recognizable. Each photograph shows one page from a series of documents in Arabic, and I've only just had the documents translated. They give the full details for Nasser's proposed plans of attack if hostilities should ever be openly renewed with Israel."

Veronica stared and then said in a hushed voice. "No wonder the Israelies were so keen to get hold of them. Schererzade must have known in general what the documents contained, but I suppose that without the photographs she couldn't possibly remember all the details."

Jackson nodded. "That's about it, but how she managed to get them with an ordinary 35 millimetre camera is beyond me! The real professionals have been using micro-cameras for almost as long as I can remember."

To Roger it seemed incredible, and he asked slowly.

"What will happen now? Will Egypt still make war on Israel?"

"I doubt it. These plans were prepared in readiness for any excuse that might have given the Egyptians the opportunity to launch an attack, but in actual fact they've been shouting about war with Israel ever since '56 and Suez and they still haven't got round to it yet. I think that just lately they've come to realize just how much the influence of Russian threats and American cowardice caused us to withdraw from the Suez fiasco. The charade of being glorious freedom fighters defeating the wicked British Empire all on their own is all very well, but they are still not willing to risk another outright battle with anybody."

Roger digested this dubiously, and asked.

"And what about the film — Schererzade's photographs."

"I don't suppose that we shall make a lot of fuss about them," Jackson said wryly. "They'll be useful of course. We can drop a hint to the Israelies to let them know which of their defences to strengthen, and after that and a subtle behind-the-scenes warning to Nasser to point out that we know what he's up to, then the Middle East should remain nicely stablized again."

They both looked disappointed. Veronica said.

"Is that all, nothing — nothing definite?"

Jackson smiled. "I'm sorry, Mrs Stewart, but that's the way that it usually is. I'm afraid the James-Bond cult has boosted the false impression that every spy case is a desperate battle to save the world from total destruction, but it's not so. Mostly we just manage to maintain the balance of international tensions."

Her eyes still mirrored disillusion, and he leaned forward and smiled again as he patted her knee.

"Cheer up, you both did a very good job even if it didn't turn out to be completely world shattering. For one thing, if those Israeli agents had got their hands on the film then Israel would have had the excuse that she needs to *attack Egypt*, if she had been so inclined. So even now you may have prevented a war. And if the Egyptians had retrieved the film then she would have been still in a position to put that attack plan into effect if the opportunity had materialized, whereas now they can't because we could always prove pre-planned aggression by publishing Shererzade's photographs to the world." He leaned back and smiled expansively. "Right now the whole situation is very nicely under our control, and I'm very grateful to you both."

Roger and Veronica smiled back at him now that they knew that their troubles had not been wholly for nothing, but then Roger's smile abruptly faded and he asked.

"What about David and Jean, the two students who vanished from the train to Luxor — and Shererzade herself — Can you do anything for them?"

Jackson too became sombre. "I don't think that there's anything that we can do for your student friends," he said gravely. "From the way you've told your story I would assume that they must have fallen foul of those Israeli agents, and as they haven't reappeared yet they are most certainly dead. I'll get the British Embassy in Cairo to instigate some enquiries, but I don't have any hopes.

"On the other hand, Schererzade is a different matter. She's still alive, and a young woman with her talents would be useful here in Aden — or a dozen other Middle Eastern cities for that matter. I could plant her in quite a lot of places where she could earn her keep, provided she can still dance of course." He paused and added. "And even if she cannot, I'd still like to help her. We may not have had any dealings lately, but I was her first paymaster. She was very young then, and contrary to all the principles of my trade I do suffer occasional pangs of conscience over the unfortunates whom I am obliged to drag into its clutches."

Veronica said hopefully. "You mean that you'll try and get her out of Egypt?"

Jackson smiled. "Not me, exactly. I'm getting a little too old for those sort of tricks. But I do happen to have a young man kicking his heels around the premises who *might* like to have a shot at it."

17

Reprieve for a Spy

The man whom Jackson had in mind was a young French-Egyptian named Kerim Soiron, for although the two had never met Soiron did have one thing in common with Schererzade. That was that he too had been charged by the Egyptians with spying. In his case the charge was also true, but Soiron had made good his own escape, and after some hectic adventures in Morocco,[1] followed by a period of convalescing after a bullet wound, he was now temporarily unemployed. However, the dust of his own escapades had settled, and as he knew Cairo intimately he was the ideal man for the job. On receiving word from

---

[1] See *Murder in Marrakech*

Jackson he accepted it immediately.

Soiron was then in Beirut, but he swiftly booked a plane flight to Alexandria where his latest passport passed scrutiny without any comment. He hired a fast car and in a little over three hours he was in Cairo. Recruiting enough of his old contacts to help him and then arranging the final details of his plans occupied him for the next two days.

★ ★ ★

Schererzade was slowly growing stronger, but daily as her condition improved so her fears increased, the fear that at any moment the police would arrive to have her transported from the hospital to a prison. She had not seen Faizal Hassain for several days, and knew that as yet he must have failed to recapture the young English couple with the film. If it had been otherwise he would have come to gloat. But even so she felt that it was only a matter of time.

Several times she had tried to rise from her bed, but although her broken bones were mending she could still move only the upper half of her body, and she succeeded only in causing herself waves of agony. The last time the nurse had noticed her sweat-drenched face and she had been severely reprimanded.

Now she had given up her attempts to lift herself from the bed, and it was late afternoon when the sound of her bedroom door being opened woke her from a drowsy sleep. The man who came towards her was not one of her regular doctors, even though he wore the usual white coat, and she was gripped by the immediate fear that her transfer to jail had come at last. The fear became even more real when she saw that there was a second man with a stretcher, and behind him a strange nurse whom she had not seen before.

Then the first man was standing over her, and she saw a pair of steel-sharp eyes and a strangely ageless face that was neither European nor full-blooded Egyptian. The man smiled and said softly.

"Trust me, Schererzade. You must not

be alarmed. Your English friends have escaped from Egypt with your precious film, and an old friend of yours named Jackson still remembers you."

The girl in the nurse's uniform was watching the door, and the second man was swiftly unfolding the stretcher as Soiron added.

"I trust that you can be moved?"

Schererzade nodded weakly, still incapable of speech, and from then on events took on the hazy non-continuity of a broken dream. She was lifted on to the stretcher, still wrapped in some of her bedsheets, and there was a spasm of pain that drove her to the very edge of unconsciousness. After that she was floating, or so it seemed, for she was passing beneath the white-painted ceilings of endless antiseptic-smelling corridors. Once there was a pause and she heard voices, but they were very far away and did not penetrate, and soon they were moving on. And then there was sudden, blinding sunlight, the first she had seen for many days, and she had to close her eyes completely against the fearsome glare. She felt herself being lifted, and she was in shadow again. Her stretcher was lowered and she heard doors being closed which made the shadow deeper. An engine started, and the vehicle that carried her began to move.

She opened her eyes, saw that she was inside an ambulance and that the girl in the nurse's uniform was still beside her. The girl was telling her softly to be still and there was no sign of the man with the ageless face, nor of the second stretcher bearer. Schererzade assumed that they must be driving and then closed her eyes and quietly fainted.

She swam back to consciousness when the ambulance stopped and again her stretcher was lifted up and carried outside. They were in a large warehouse of some kind and a large car was waiting to receive her. It was a wide American station waggon and there was plenty of room for her stretcher to lay crossways in the back.

She had a vague impression of two tubby little men in their underwear being hustled out of a darkened corner and shoved into the back of the ambulance she had just left. Both of them were tightly bound with ropes and were muffled with gags and blindfolds. The doors were slammed and the ambulance quickly drove off, back into the streets of Cairo.

The girl who had been watching her moved away, and a moment later that reassuring ageless face was smiling down at her again. The man had got rid of his white coat and now looked handsome in a smart lightweight suit.

Soiron said casually. "That is it, Schererzade, the worst part is over. Getting you out of the hospital was my biggest problem, but I reasoned that providing the police were not actually mounting a guard over you then broad daylight and the busiest part of the day would be the best time. And you see, I was right. The police knew you could not move, and obviously the last thing they expected was that anyone would try to rescue you. They do not credit the British with hearts, although I must confess that I think your future usefulness must have been the biggest factor in deciding Jackson to pull you out."

Schererzade said feebly. "I don't understand."

"Perhaps not, but don't worry. My friend will drive the ambulance that we were obliged to borrow into some lonely back street, and by the time the genuine driver and his colleague have extracted themselves from their bonds in the back you and I will be well clear of Cairo."

"But — but where are we going?"

"To Alexandria. There, after nightfall, you will be transferred to a fishing boat, which will take us far out into the Mediterranean. There it will rendezvous with a second boat which will take us to Cyprus. And there you will be safe."

The girl returned, and Schererzade saw that she had now changed from her fake nurse's uniform and wore a simple cotton frock. Soiron said briefly.

"This is Selina, she is a good friend of mine and she has had nursing experience. She will ride with us and look after you until we sail from Alexandria. My name is Kerim."

Selina smiled reassuringly, and then climbed into the back of the station waggon to sit on a cushion beside the stretcher. Kerim Soiron closed the back doors, and then moved around the car to slide behind the driving wheel. He started the engine and he was humming a blithe tune as he engaged the clutch and drove out of the warehouse. Behind him Schererzade could hardly believe her good fortune, for already the strange foresight that she had derived from the blood of her mother was returning, and she knew instinctively that she could trust this man, and that at last her period of danger was almost over.

★ ★ ★

However, even though Schererzade had been successfully reprieved, the same was not so for Roger and Veronica. They were still in Aden, for Jackson's promise of a flight home was very much a question of availability, and so far there had been no vacant seats on any of the routine R.A.F. flights to England. In the meantime they had been installed in one of Aden's best hotels and were making the best of it. They had seen practically nothing more of Jackson himself, but the friendly Inspector Bartlett had stopped by from time to time, to ensure that they were behaving themselves he had cheerfully explained.

This was now their third night since they had been landed from the *Judith Rose*, and although they had happily renewed the delights of their interrupted honeymoon, they were becoming tired of the delay. The close confines of the hotel were proving a strain, for Aden was a restricted town with British troops patrolling the streets to guard against any outbreaks of terrorism and violence. They were not exactly forbidden to go out into the streets, but after their past experiences neither of them were inclined to take any risks.

Fortunately Roger still had quite a bit of his money left and so they were able to buy a plentiful supply of iced drinks and magazines to while away the time. The room service was prompt and efficient and he had fallen into the habit of calling down frequently for fresh ice. The heat was such that even in the evenings ice was more of a necessity than a luxury, and at approximately the same moment that Schererzade was being successfully smuggled aboard the fishing boat in Alexandria harbour, Roger picked up the telephone and made the routine call.

It was Veronica who went to the door a few minutes later, and a white-coated waiter with a dark blue tarboosh entered carrying the tray. He was not their usual waiter, but the fact did not strike Roger immediately. What did register was the fact that his order had been confused. He said promptly.

"That's not what I asked for!"

The waiter looked uncertainly at his tray.

"But this is your usual order, sir. One whisky-soda — One dry-martini — Plenty ice."

"I know," Roger said wearily. "But this time I only asked for the ice. We've got all the other stuff up here, and in any case I wanted the ice to put in some lemonade."

The waiter looked crestfallen and stood there doubtfully with his tray. Then Veronica said sympathetically.

"It doesn't matter, we'll have them anyway." She took the two prepared drinks and added. "Just go back and bring us some more ice."

The waiter nodded thankfully and hurried away, and then she turned to face Roger's disapproving gaze.

"Women!" he said. "No wonder they always get exploited. You're too soft-hearted."

"Don't be such a bully," she responded. "He was a new boy, and he's probably just a learner. We all make mistakes — and I'll bet that you would have mixed one of these anyway."

She handed him the whisky and soda and he accepted gracefully.

"Here's to beautiful, softhearted women," he toasted.

"And to horrible, bullying men."

They drank, and then carried the glasses back to the armchair where they had both been sitting. Roger sat on the arm and rattled the ice in his glass, he watched the amber liquid swirl around the chunky cubes and then he carefully finished it off. Veronica was still sipping her martini as she picked up the magazine she had been reading and spread it upon her lap. Roger looked over her shoulder and noticed that the print was blurred on the magazine's pages, and that Veronica seemed to be having difficulty in turning them over. He felt strangely dizzy and Veronica began to dissolve into a haze in front of him.

Their eyes met and he said harshly.

"Ronnie — "

"Roger."

Her face was sick and frightened and the glass tumbled from her fingers as she reached towards him. She tried to stand and abruptly sprawled sideways off the chair.

Roger wanted to go to her, but his limbs were like lead, and to preserve his balance he had to stay still. The whole room tilted into a whirl of slow motion, and the passing door gently opened. The strange waiter smiled as he joined the dimly spinning furniture and Roger swore. He tried to reach the laughing figure and crashed headlong upon the floor.

From far above his head a mocking voice expressed its soft apologies, and explained that Major Faizal Hassain had a very earnest desire to meet them both at least once more.

18

The Lair of the Red Wolves

The first thing of which Roger was aware when he ultimately recovered consciousness was the violent, aching pain that filled the whole of his head and spread down to engulf the back of his neck. The second thing was that something underneath him was lurching and pitching with crazy irregularity, chafing at his thighs and thrusting at his bottom. Finally there was the dryness of his mouth, the sweating heat of the sun, and the fact that his hands were lashed at the wrists in front of him.

He opened his eyes and saw that his wrists were secured to the polished wooden pommel of a strange bulky saddle, and that beyond them was the long, swaying neck of a camel. He blinked, and then closed his eyes against the throbbing of his head. The back of the camel gave a humped lurch and he swayed sideways, but his feet were tied somewhere to the saddle harness and a rough hand beside him propped the top half of his body upright once more.

It took a few minutes for his headache to become bearable, but then he made an effort to establish his surroundings. He was trussed neatly to the back of a camel somewhere in the South Arabian desert, and on either side of him were two more camel-riders who were pressing close enough to support him whenever he showed signs of toppling to one side. His two guards were both wild-looking men wearing ragged robes and turbans, and both of them were burdened down with gleaming rifles, ammunition pouches and big-handled knives. Ahead of them rode several more camels in single file, most of them pack animals but some with riders. The camel directly ahead again had a limp figure tied to the saddle between two mounted guards, and although only her bowed back was visible Roger recognized the new dove-grey dress that Veronica had bought for herself in Aden.

He tried to see farther, but there was nothing around them but barren stony rocks, and ahead a rising tangle of bleak, sun-glaring mountains. The blistering heat was almost as bad as it had been in the Red Sea, and from the height of the sun he knew that it must be past noon. Mercifully his captors had thought to tie an old turban around his head to protect him from sunstroke, but even so he felt more dead than alive.

He looked uncertainly at his nearest neighbour and the man grinned at him widely. His face had the colour and texture of an old, dark brown boot, and his teeth ranged from yellow to brown with one jet black stump that was isolated from the rest. He spoke casually to his companion to indicate that their prisoner was awake.

Roger said harshly.

"What the hell is all this? Where are you taking us?"

The tribesman merely shrugged, a universal gesture of non-comprehension, and he grinned more widely. Roger felt rising anger, but then a rough hand twisted him round. The second guard looked even less friendly than the first, even though his teeth were possibly in a little better condition. He too was grinning and from his belt he pulled his big-handled knife. It had a long, curved blade that gleamed like molten silver as he moved it to catch the sun. He touched his thumb along the edge and then made a meaningful gesture of drawing the blade across Roger's throat. Instinctively Roger flinched away and the two men laughed with almost childish delight. Somewhat reluctantly the man with knife thrust it back into his belt, but for a long time they continued to chuckle and exchange amused glances.

After that Roger remained silent, for it was clear that even if his present captors could understand English they were still not inclined to enlighten him about his fate. He had realized by now that the last drinks they had been given back at the hotel had been drugged, and he vaguely remembered the fake waiter mentioning

315

the name of Faizal Hassain. From that he could only deduce that they were once again in the Egyptian Major's clutches, and that he would be waiting for them at their journey's end. The thought was not a pleasant one, and he looked upon the coming meeting with a loose, watery feeling in the pit of his stomach.

For the next three hours the slowly-plodding camel train moved into the grim wilderness of cliffs and boulders. The bare peaks made a forbidding barrier against the sharp blue of the sky, and many of the deep ravines they followed trapped the heat like natural ovens. The white-hot sun continued to rule this fierce wasteland with unabated power, and Roger felt once more as though he must surely die from heat exhaustion. He had no desire to face Faizal Hassain again, but even so he prayed that the journey would soon be over.

Ahead of him Veronica had also recovered from the effects of her doped drink, for her back had straightened a little and once or twice she had attempted to look back towards him. The thought of her fate troubled him more than his own, but there was nothing that he could do to comfort her.

He was feeling utterly deflated when at last they showed signs of approaching their destination. The camel train had moved into a large ravine that appeared to be in the very heart of the mountain range, and at the far end the ravine widened out to make room for a scattering of ruined stone houses, interspaced with a ramshackle collection of tents. More savage, wild-eyed men appeared to meet them, and like the men with the camel train each one was adorned with ammunition pouches and knives, and each one carried a bright shining rifle. They were a ragged, formidable crew, and as they emerged from their tents they stood silently waiting.

Roger looked slowly around the bleak cliff walls that towered upwards on three sides, and then saw that they were not quite as barren as he had first supposed. They were spotted with caves, and here and there there were signs that the larger ones were in use. His attention came back to earth as his camel was pulled to a stop by a man on his right who held the reins, and he looked reluctantly forward.

The whole camel train had stopped, and an old man with a grizzled grey beard and a flowing burnous secured by a gold band across his lined temples had walked out slowly to meet them. He too carried a rifle, cradled in the crook of his arm, but he also carried authority. He spoke briefly with the mounted men at the head of the line of camels, and his interest appeared to be wholly devoted to the pack animals. His dark brown face showed grim satisfaction and after some discussion he turned to pass some orders to the nearest of the waiting men behind him. The men addressed ran swiftly forward to take the reins of the five pack camels and led them away.

Roger had not previously taken any notice of the burdens that the camels were carrying, but now as they were led past him he saw that each beast had a long wooden box strapped to either side of its hump instead of the

318

usual laden panniers. He automatically thought of arms and ammunition, for the wooden crates looked to be about the right size, and he watched as the camels were led towards the mouth of a large cave in the cliff wall. Then his attention was diverted as his own camel was driven forward.

For the first time he was immediately beside Veronica, and he saw that she too looked very much in despair. She sat astride her camel painfully, and her bare knees looked badly sunburned below the level of her crumpled dress. She looked at him hopelessly, and her large hazel eyes were near to tears beneath the clumsy turban they had given her.

"Roger — what has happened?"

"Our drinks were drugged," he answered wearily. "I only know that Major Hassain is responsible."

They became aware then that the old grey-bearded Arab was glaring up at them, and they were chilled into silence by his hawk-like eyes. He was very obviously the leader of the band of disreputable ruffians who surrounded him, and after a moment he stepped back and gave an order.

Their captors from the camel train had dismounted by now, and Roger's two guards instantly drew their knives. His body tensed but they merely grinned as they slashed the ropes that bound him to the camel's back. Two sharp thwacks from a rifle butt, first at the neck and then at the rump, caused the camel to lean forward and then settle itself slowly on the sandy ground, and Roger was pulled off and on to his feet.

Veronica's camel was also kneeling, and with an angry shove Roger pushed aside his two guards and went to help her. Their grins darkened, but the grey-bearded Arab gave them no sign and so they did not interfere. Roger helped Veronica to stand and for a moment she pressed into his arms.

"Are you all right?" he asked hoarsely.

"I think so." Her voice was very unsteady. "My head aches and I feel sick, but I think that's all."

Roger put his arm around her, and then turned to face the tattered brigands who had closed around them. All of them were as fearsome and unwholesome as the grinning villain who had mimed the promise of slitting his throat, and there was over a score in number. The older man with the short grey beard and the white burnous was the only one who did not look completely illiterate. Roger met his gaze slowly, and then saw that their real enemy had at last appeared and was standing at the old man's side.

Major Faizal Hassain was no longer wearing the dark, sombre suit which he usually favoured, and instead he had exchanged it for grey desert robes and a grey burnous that was secured across his forehead. He was an inch or two taller than the old Arab chieftain, and although he carried no visible weapons he looked the more deadly of the two. His thin, sly face wore an almost lipless smile, and there was a glitter of triumph in his deep-set eyes.

"Mr and Mrs Stewart," he said softly. "It was so nice of you to come. I trust that you had a pleasant journey?"

Roger ignored the honeyed malice and

demanded bluntly.

"Where the hell are we? Why have we been brought here?"

Hassain said calmly. "I thought that you might have guessed where you are, but if not I shall tell you. You are about seventy-five miles from Aden, in the Radfan Mountain Range that runs close to the Yemen border. It is an area that your countrymen have found to be somewhat hazardous, and indeed they have labelled these hills as being infested with terrorists."

"Radfan — " Roger repeated slowly. He didn't finish, but stared round at the fierce circle of faces and the dark, watchful eyes.

Hassain nodded. "That is right my young friend. These excellent fellows you see around you are some of the bloodthirsty mountain tribesmen whom you call the Red Wolves!"

There was a pause of silence, and then Veronica said helplessly. "But I still don't understand. What are you doing here? And why have we been brought here?"

"It is all very simple, my dear." Hassain

explained to her with sly pleasure. "I knew that you had reached Aden, for the ship that picked you up from the Red Sea was obliged to acknowledge the fact to the Egyptian authorities, and so I begged a few days leave of my duties to settle the small personal matters that still exist between us. Fortunately Egyptian influence is very strong in the Yemen and so I was able to fly there in the company of some of their freedom fighters whom we have recently been training in Egypt. With their help I was then able to cross the border into this part of the Aden Protectorate and contact these noble Red Wolves. Their co-operation was easily acquired, for they loathe the British and it is my country that provides most of their arms."

He smiled. "But of course, you are still wondering just how was I able to spirit you away from your hotel room, from under the very noses of your own police. The answer again is one of great simplicity, for as a Major of one of Egypt's intelligence departments I hold a great amount of personal influence.

The man who took the place of the waiter at your hotel was, as you must have guessed, an Egyptian agent. He gave you a very strong drug, and with the help of a colleague carried you down the back stairs of the hotel to a waiting truck. You were driven out of Aden on the road that crosses the Yemen frontier and continues on to Taiz, but before reaching the frontier the truck turned off the road to meet this camel train. They were bound for this village with the boxes you saw unloaded, and they came by a roundabout route to avoid the British patrols that are engaged in fighting what they prefer to call the rebels in this area."

Roger had listened in silence, but now he said truculently.

"All right, so you've been very clever and now you've caught us — but I don't see what good it's going to do you. We haven't got Schererzade's roll of film any more. It has already been developed by one of *our* intelligence departments, and they now know what's in it."

Hassain nodded slowly. "I have realized

324

that. It is unfortunate but I must admit defeat upon that aspect of the affair. However, I believe I did mention that this is a personal score — or have you forgotten that Kamal Hassain, the young Police Inspector whom you killed at Quseir, was my brother?"

Roger paled and said hesitantly. "But that was an accident. I did fight with your brother, but he struck his head on a boat's anchor that was half buried in the sand. I didn't see the blasted thing until it was too late. I didn't kill him deliberately."

"Deliberately or not, you *did* kill him." Hassain's tone had not changed but his eyes glittered more darkly. He went on. "I am not normally an emotional man Mr Stewart. In my chosen profession I cannot afford to be. But I was fond of Kamal — he was my younger brother, my only brother, in fact my only living relative. We were very close."

Veronica pressed close to Roger's side and said in a low voice.

"Then you intend to take us back to Egypt?"

"No, my dear," Hassain replied calmly. "I have already decided that you shall die, and your execution can most suitably take place on this very spot."

It was no more than Roger had expected, but from the manner in which her body had stiffened at his side he knew that to Veronica it had come as a shock. He knew that delay could only extend the agony and tightening his arm around her he said savagely.

"All right you murdering sod, get it over with. You can save yourself any further trouble by shooting us right now."

"Please," Hassain said plaintively. "One cannot rush into these things just like that. If I had wanted you to be simply murdered my agent in Aden could have sprinkled cyanide into your drinks instead of a mere sleeping draught. It would have saved all the bother of bringing you here. The very reason for your little journey was because there are so many limits to what can be done in a city, while here there are no ears to hear you, or eyes to see. Except the Red Wolves of course, but their hearts are not noted for any feelings of pity."

Despite the heat, and the sweat that trickled down his face, Roger felt as though the water in his stomach had turned to ice. He drew a deep breath, and it took an effort of will to ask.

"What do you intend to do with us?"

The Egyptian Major smiled slyly. "Something a little more dramatic I think — more frightening perhaps than mere shooting. You may remember that some of your more excitable newspapers reported that two British soldiers had been beheaded in these mountains a short while ago. Now I am not going to comment on whether those reports may have been true, but with the Red Wolves it is not impossible and the idea strikes me as an excellent way of arranging your own executions."

Roger felt a wave of revulsion and horror.

"Damn it, man, you can't let them do that! You're supposed to be civilized, even if they are not."

"That is irrelevant," Hassain said

bitingly. "And Kamal was my *only* brother. I feel that you must suffer more than he did before he can be fully avenged."

Roger stared round helplessly at the silent faces of the watching tribesmen. The rank and file of the armed rebels offered him no hope, and desperately he looked towards the cold but regal features of the grey-bearded Chieftain.

"You can't allow this," he shouted. "This is cold-blooded murder — not the heat of a battle."

"You are wasting your breath," Hassain told him bluntly. "For one thing the old Sheikh does not speak English, and for another — look around you! The stone houses of this village are nearly all in ruins. That is why they live in tents, and there are no women and children. Once this was not a rebel stronghold, but some of your R.A.F. planes made the mistake of believing that it was. They bombed it thoroughly. Now those who survived *are* rebels, and they *have* made a stronghold out of what remains. The memory of the bombing, and of the wives and children that many of them lost, has made them hate the British with more passion than most of the other tribesmen even in these embittered hills. The Sheikh lost his own wife in that clumsy bombing raid, and if it were not beneath his dignity I think that he would personally wield the sword that will sever your heads from your necks."

Veronica had listened to every word, and despite her fear she said feebly.

"I still don't believe it, no matter what you say. They can't be that barbaric!"

Hassain laughed. "They would not understand the meaning of the word barbaric. You must realize that here values and customs are very different to your polite England. Beheading is an old and much-favoured form of Arab execution. They will be pleased to see it revived."

Roger swore, he had heard enough and thrusting himself forward he aimed a savage blow at Hassain's loathsome face. The Major merely smiled and stepped back, while the tribesmen around him sprang swiftly forward. Roger and Veronica were seized, and after a few scuffling moments subdued.

Roger was panting hard and bleeding from a vicious cut across the face when he gave up the unequal struggle. His arms were pinioned behind his back by two of the armed rebels, and Veronica, her face stained with grief and anguish, was similarly held. Hassain regarded them with sly tolerance, and then glanced around the barrier of cliffs that enclosed the wide ravine. Their shadows were long and the sun was already touching the tops of the highest peaks. He observed all this, and then said.

"In a few moments the sun will have set, and as the traditional time for an execution is at dawn I shall give you one last night of life to dwell upon your past mistakes. I am in no hurry, and I would prefer that your mental agony be drawn out as long as possible."

He smiled at them both, and then added.

"However, there is one last, subtle refinement. I see no need to let the two of you spend your last night together.

But, Mr Stewart, your young wife is such a sweet and bedworthy little thing that it grieves me to think that she should be alone. Therefore out of kindness she will spend her last night with me."

19

Night of Terror

For the next few moments Roger Stewart went totally insane. He hurled off the two men who were holding him and he was half way towards Faizal Hassain before the mass of the Red Wolves could rush in to restrain him. He fought them with blind, tigerish rage, cursing, kicking and clawing in his efforts to get his hands upon the throat of the Egyptian Major. It took six of the struggling tribesmen to hold him down, and even then it needed a rifle butt driven with sickening force into his stomach to force him to his knees. He slumped forward, gagging helplessly with his face close to the sand, and then a lighter, more methodical tap from the rifle smacked against the side of his head to render him half insensible.

Two yards away Veronica twisted and sobbed in the hard grip of her captors but was unable to break free and help him. While Hassain watched them both with placid amusement, the glitter in his deep-set eyes showing the full extent of the pleasure he derived from the scene. He waited until they had both been subdued and then said quietly.

"I judged you well, Mr Stewart. I guessed from your previous reactions whenever your young bride has been threatened that this would be the finest torture that I could devise. Only a man who was fully in love with his wife would have made that stupid jump through the temple roof at Karnak, and then taken on the whole of the Egyptian police force to save her from a simple prison sentence. Your response has been most gratifying."

Roger made no answer, for the blow in the stomach had winded him cruelly and he could barely breathe. But he was just conscious and the sick fury in his eyes as he weakly lifted his head gave Hassain the satisfaction he needed.

The Major smiled and went on. "I can assure you that I will give good service to your precious bride, and you will be reunited at dawn in order to die together. Meanwhile we do have one stone hut that has survived the bombing, which will make a suitable cell where you can spend the night in solitary meditation. The agony of the mind is so much more acute than the agony of the body — wouldn't you agree?"

Roger was still incapable of speech, and after a pause Hassain turned to the old Chieftain who had watched with a blank face and impassive eyes. He spoke briefly and the grey-bearded Arab nodded and waved an authoritative hand towards his followers. He continued to watch with the same impersonal detachment as Roger was lifted up and carried away.

Roger was unable to resist as he was half dragged through the untidy jumble of tents and ruined stone walls. A stray dog and a bleating goat were kicked from their path by the group of wild men who held him and finally he was pushed into a small square hut that was solidly built of stone. He was thrust face down on to the bare floor and subjected to laughing comments and a barrage of kicks before he was left alone. The heavy wooden door was slammed and barred behind him, and for a long time he lay in a crumpled heap.

When at last he was able to move it was dark, and he pushed himself feebly into a sitting position. He stayed there for a moment, and then twisted round to prop his back against the wall. His head was aching sorely and when he explored with his fingers he could feel the drying blood upon his face. His stomach still hurt and the first time he tried to move he retched, drawing spasms of fresh pain from the bruised muscles.

He lay against the wall and looked slowly around him. The hut was small, about ten feet square, and he guessed that it had been one room of a larger building before the outer walls had been demolished around it. There was only one window, which was about a foot square and set at head height. The door looked strong enough to withstand a charging elephant and the walls appeared to be a good ten inches thick.

In one corner was an earthenware jar. It was the only thing in the room and as the darkness was only relieved by the dim moonlight from the window it was a long time before he noticed it in the gloom. The long neck and squat body of the jar suggested a possible weapon, and he crawled to reach it. He lifted it by the neck to check its suitability as a club, and to his surprise found that it was full of water.

He didn't understand, but he drank deeply and then used what was left to wash the blood from his face. The cool water revived him a little and with an effort he was able to stand.

At first he thought that the water-jar must have been an oversight, but later he was to realize that Hassain had provided it with careful forethought. For without the water to sharpen his senses he might have spent the night semi-conscious on the floor, too doped from hurt and thirst to be able to think clearly. And Hassain wanted him to think. Hassain wanted his mind to remain clear enough to picture vividly the unseen sufferings of his wife.

Roger stumbled over to the small window, but he could only see the ragged outlines of the armed tribesmen around the dancing fires that were now scattered among the walls and tents. There was no sign of either Hassain or Veronica, and he could only imagine where they might be and what might be taking place. The window was too small for him to squeeze through, and when he went to the door a crack between its heavy boards showed him that a rifle-bristling guard was squatting watchfully outside. He turned away and in desperation began clawing at the walls, hoping to find a cracked or weakened spot where he could insert his fingers and tear at the heavy stones with his bare hands. He tore his nails and knuckles, but it was all futile and there was no way out.

★ ★ ★

Veronica was forced to watch as her beaten husband was dragged away and thrown into the stone hut that was to be his cell, and then she turned her gaze towards Faizal Hassain.

"You're an animal," she told him hysterically. "You're nothing but a filthy, uncivilized animal!"

Hassain smiled. "Then you should be well pleased, my dear. For animals make the best lovers, they have no inhibitions." He chuckled and finished. "But it is early yet, and I shall not want you until I have eaten and am ready to retire for the night. Until then we must find you some separate place of confinement, where you too can dwell upon what is left of your future."

He turned to speak once more with the Arab Chieftain, and the old man nodded in careless agreement. Veronica was immediately hustled forward and pushed into one of the larger tents. A calloused hand thrust her down on to the rich blue carpet that covered the floor, and her wrists were deftly lashed to one of the main supporting poles. The two ruffians who had secured her grinned obscenely, and made definite gestures to indicate what was in store for her before they went away.

When she was alone Veronica tugged desperately at her ropes in an effort to free herself, but she succeeded only in chafing her wrists until the ropes drew blood. She gave up then, and after a few moments of dull despair she finally lifted her head and tried to establish her surroundings.

Outside it was night, but the door flap of the tent had been left open and a flickering glow from the fires that had now been lit outside enabled her to distinguish the main shapes around her. The big tent was built in the shape of a square around four main poles, and the floor was covered with rugs, carpets and cushions. There was a low divan and several small tables. The comparative luxury of the furnishings suggested that it was the tent of the Sheikh himself, and this fact served to strengthen Veronica's despair. For if the Sheikh had vacated his tent in favour of Hassain then it showed that the Egyptian Major was in absolute control.

Through the open doorflap she could see the grim silhouettes of the tribesmen squatting, or moving idly among their fires. Beyond lay the black ramparts of the cliffs that enclosed the wide ravine, and between two soaring peaks there was a lighter V of star-bright sky. The night air was becoming cooler and a faint breeze carried the stench of camels and the aroma of stewing meat.

For several hours no one came near her, and Veronica was able to rally some of her failing courage. She could see no escape, and so she steeled herself to face whatever was to come. She waited, feeling sick inside, but at least she had regained a few shreds of self-control. And then her nerves jumped with fresh terror at the sound of movements outside the tent.

Faizal Hassain blocked the entrance. His face was invisible in the darkness, but apart from the old Sheikh he was the only one of their captors to wear a flowing burnous, and that and his height marked him clearly. He moved to the nearer of the supporting poles and a match sparked in his cupped hands. By its tiny flame Veronica saw that he was lighting a large oil lamp that hung from the pole, and in the increasing light his face became slowly visible.

Two of the rebels entered behind him, and placed some dishes, a water jar and a wine bottle on one of the tables. They grinned at Veronica and then hurried away. Hassain pulled down the doorflap and secured it behind them.

He turned back and smiled at the crouching girl on the floor. Casually he unfastened the burnous from around his temples and tossed it aside. He took off the long grey desert robe and underneath he was wearing dark trousers and a white shirt. He smoothed back his black hair and then moved calmly towards her.

Veronica flinched as he drew a knife from his pocket and snapped open the blade. He cut through the ropes that bound her to the tent pole and she immediately squirmed away.

"Please," Hassain said calmly. "You must not show so much revulsion." He reached for her arm and his hard fingers half lifted and half dragged her to her feet. "I have eaten," he continued. "But I have not forgotten you entirely. There is food and drink upon the table."

She glared at him rebelliously.

"What about Roger?"

"I have provided for Roger," Hassain assured her. "I had a full jar of water placed in his cell. After all, I do want him to survive until dawn." He dismissed the subject and went on. "The food in the dishes is stewed goat's flesh. It is not exactly what you would get in the Nile Hilton, but it is the best that we can provide."

She said weakly. "I'm not hungry."

"Ah I see! You are impatient for our lovemaking to begin."

Veronica hesitated, and then moved slowly to the table that held the food. She knew that Hassain was playing with her, like a cat pawing gently at a mouse, but even to delay the inevitable she could not bring herself to swallow the greasy chunks of stewed goat. However, the inside of her mouth tasted like yellowed parchment and she reached for the water jar with both hands.

Hassain watched her drink and said casually.

"By the way, I have some news for you. Your two friends whom you left at Quseir — the Israeli agent and his Arab companion — They have been sentenced to death for the murder of Sergeant Kalman. I hope that makes you happy."

For once Hassain's remarks missed their intended effect, for Veronica lowered the water jar and said bluntly.

"It does make me happy. They were no friends of ours, and anyway they murdered two students who were our friends."

Hassain sighed, and then removed the water jar from her hands before it occurred to her to use it as a weapon. He replaced it on the table, and then changed the tone of his conversation.

"You are very attractive," he said softly. "Did you know that? It is a pity that you have been weeping for it stains a very lovely face. This is a fighting stronghold, and unfortunately the men here do not have their womenfolk with them, otherwise I could have sent you some Arab girls to restore your former beauty."

She backed away and said harshly.

"I wouldn't have let them touch me!"

"Oh come now, Ronnie, surely you would have preferred to be at your most beautiful for your last lover." He smiled. "I trust that you will not object if I call you Ronnie. I believe it is the intimate term that your husband is inclined to use, so perhaps it will put you at your ease."

Veronica said nothing, and calmly Hassain stripped off his white shirt, revealing a dark chest that was thickly tangled with jet black hair.

"If you do not wish to eat," he said simply. "Then we may as well begin."

Veronica could feel her heart thudding and her knees felt weak and unstable as she took another step backwards.

"If you touch me I'll claw your eyes out!"

Hassain chuckled. "You please me, Ronnie. I prefer a woman who will struggle. Rape is so much more pleasurable than seduction, and the cost of a few scratches means nothing against the ultimate triumph of victory. Please do not take your clothes off — I would much rather tear them from your back."

He lunged towards her and her flailing nails raked desperately at his face. She missed his eyes but scored red streaks along his cheek before he could close with her and pin her arms to her sides. She fought with every nerve and muscle, twisting and writhing in his bear-hugging grasp, and bodily she was carried backwards until her shoulders struck against the tent pole. Hassain was smiling delightedly and his dark eyes glittered with feverish brilliance as he included the pole in his embrace and crushed her against it. She tried to avoid his hungry mouth but inevitably he found her lips as his fingers knotted in her chestnut hair to hold her still.

She felt his tongue thrusting against her clenched mouth, and in a frenzy of revulsion she almost broke free. She slipped away from the tent pole and fell sideways, sprawling on to the deep blue carpet with Hassain crashing on top of her. The impact drove the breath from her lungs and for a moment she was helpless as he held her down. Her legs moved feebly as he pushed her dress above her hips and thighs, and grabbing a handful of the material at her waist he endeavoured to tear it from her squirming body. She heard it rip as she struggled to push his remaining hand from her breast, and then abruptly there was an interruption.

Hassain swore as he heard the curt voice from outside the tent, and slowly he pushed himself upright. He went to the door and jerked the tent-flap partially open. Veronica could not see who was there but she recognized the voice of the old Arab Sheikh.

She got up slowly as the two men argued in the doorway, and leaned against the tent-pole until her breathing had started to approach normal. Her whole body was violently trembling and she smoothed down her dishevelled dress with shaking hands.

The argument lasted several minutes,

and although it was conducted in Arabic the tone of the voices showed that the angry Hassain was winning. She realized that within moments the old Arab would go away, and that then nothing could save her from being raped by the tall Major. Nothing that is, except her own resources. She looked round frantically for a weapon and her gaze found the wine bottle that had been left on the table with the unwanted food.

Hassain's back was towards her, and the Sheikh was still out of sight as she made her move. She held her breath and her feet made no sound on the deeply piled carpets as she crossed in three long strides to the table. She picked up the bottle and returned as silently to her original position. Despite her trembling her mind was functioning clearly and she thrust the bottle out of sight behind her. She pressed her spine against it to hold it against the pole, and stood with both her hands visible and empty.

She was only just in time, for the old Sheikh had made his final point and turned away, and Hassain was swiftly refastening the tent-flap. He drew a deep breath as he swung back to face her, and his black-haired chest was rising and falling with slow regularity. The interruption had angered him, but again he smiled thinly.

"That was somewhat unfortunate, but I do not think we will be troubled again. The old Sheikh is somewhat worried because there is one of your British patrols in the vicinity. Presumably the camel train which brought you here must have been spotted earlier in the afternoon, and these British patrols spend most of their time chasing after camel trains to prevent arms being smuggled in from the Yemen. The Sheikh wanted to silence both you and your husband immediately so that both your bodies could be well hidden in the unlikely event of the patrol arriving here, but I have persuaded him to give us a few more hours in which to enjoy ourselves."

He came towards her and added. "You fight well, Ronnie. You have aroused me — and now you are ripe for our final embraces."

Veronica's face was pale and filmed with sweat, and she pressed back hard against the tent pole as he approached. The hard bulge of the wine bottle had slipped and was now jammed against the lower joints of her spine. She was afraid that it would fall completely but she dared not use her hands now that Hassain was facing her once more. She waited until his hands reached out to fasten on her shoulders, and then she looked behind him and shouted shrilly.

"Roger!"

It was the oldest trick in the world. Veronica had read it in a hundred stories and watched it scores of times on television and films, but it was the only one she knew. She knew it only because it was so old, and because Hassain had not credited her with any further will to resist it worked far better than she had hoped. With a trained, or even half-trained man Hassain would not have been fooled even for an instant, but with a terrified and helpless girl whom he had not expected to know even the simplest of tricks his head did twist round for one startled, vital second.

Veronica reached behind her for the neck of the bottle and swung it at his head with all the force she could muster in her arm. The movement warned Hassain but he could not deflect the clumsy, desperate blow, and the heavy bottle, still corked and full of wine, smacked solidly against his right ear. The Egyptian howled and staggered and in blind fury Veronica hit him again and clubbed him to the floor.

Hassain fell unconscious and Veronica stood over him with the unbroken bottle still in her hand. She was still terrified, and her stomach was even more jittery now than before she had struck him down. She badly wanted to be sick and she swayed dizzily before clinging to the tent pole for support. She expected the tribesmen to rush in and overpower her but nothing happened, and then her mind was filled with the all-demanding need to return to Roger.

She stumbled towards the tent-flap, but then some primitive sense of caution made her change her mind. She turned instead and made for the back of the tent, falling to her knees where the canvas wall slanted outwards. She dragged frantically at the lower edge until she had hauled up enough to make a small opening, and then she got down on her belly and wriggled out into the black night.

She stayed there, crouching, and still gripping the comforting neck of the heavy bottle. There was no one in sight and it seemed that the whole band of the Red Wolves must be gathered around the fires in front of their tents. Here there was nothing but the rubble-strewn paths and broken walls of the bombed village, with the cliffs beyond and a few stars dimly relieving the darkness above.

She remembered the direction of the hut into which Roger had been thrown, and hunching herself as low as possible she scrambled towards it. Her ears were pricked for any sound of discovery, and her pumping heart felt as though at any moment it could force its way upwards into her trembling throat. She passed the end of the large tent and wriggled on to

351

her belly once more as she passed an open space in full view of the camp fires. Mercifully most of the tribesmen seemed to be sleeping, although she guessed that somewhere there must be sentries who were awake.

It took her five, sweating, fear-filled minutes to get close to the stone hut in which Roger had been imprisoned, and then she saw that there was an armed guard sitting outside the door. The man was sitting with his elbows on his knees and appeared to be dozing, but his rifle was unslung and lying close across his thighs.

Veronica felt near to despair, but she had to make some attempt to tackle the man before she could release Roger, and so she drew deeply upon her remaining shreds of courage and strength. She inched nearer, praying that the man would not look up and holding her upraised wine bottle like a club. It seemed impossible that he could not hear the thudding tumult of her heartbeat, and when she was still ten feet away she could stand it no longer and rushed him.

The guard heard the scuff of sand and stones and jerked awake with a start. The rifle lifted in his hands and he thrust his back away from the wall behind him. His eyes were staring and his mouth opened to shout as the wine bottle descended. Then the bottle broke and flooded his face with cheap red wine as it cracked against his skull.

This time Veronica was sick as the man toppled sideways into a senseless heap. She pressed against the wall and retched, and then fumbled weakly with the door of the hut. There was no lock, but simply a massive bolt and a heavy wooden bar. She pushed them both aside and stumbled helplessly into the blessed haven of Roger's arms.

He was almost out of his mind with worry, and when the door opened and he caught her falling body he could hardly believe that she was real. He held her close and felt her shaking uncontrollably as she wept on his shoulder, and for a moment he was close to tears himself. He comforted her as best he could, kissing away her tears and caressing her until at last her trembling ceased, and then he asked the question that had agonized his mind. He tried to ask it softly for her sake, but the words came harsh and grated.

"Ronnie, did he — did he force you?"

"He tried," she said weakly. "But I hit him with a bottle. Roger, I think I've killed him."

"If you haven't then I damned well will," he said savagely.

He left her for a moment and dragged the unconscious tribesman into the hut. Swiftly he robbed the man of his ammunition pouches, the rifle and his knife, and having transferred them to his own person he felt much more capable. The rifle was unfamiliar in his hands but he checked the bolt movement and ensured that it was loaded, and if Faizal Hassain had appeared in that moment then the combined forces of God and the Devil would not have saved him from an explosive death.

Grimly Roger turned back to Veronica and asked her to tell him everything that had happened. She obeyed, and when she mentioned that there was a British patrol somewhere nearby his face showed a glimmer of hope.

"Then there's a chance," he declared. "If we can attract their attention then they might be in time to help us."

"But how?" she asked blankly.

He smiled bleakly, for the first time in twenty-four hours.

"Do you remember those big wooden crates that came in with our camel train? I'm damned sure that they must have contained arms, and therefore it follows that the cave where they were unloaded is an arms dump. If we can get to it then I reckon that British patrol will come running when I blow it sky-high!"

20

Dawn

They left the hut warily, but there was nothing to indicate that the remainder of the Red Wolves suspected anything to be wrong. Roger carefully replaced the bar across the door but the act was only a gesture and he did not really expect it to gain him any extra time. For even if the guard was not missed and the barred door fooled the tribesmen into believing that he was still safely locked inside, Roger was sure that Faizal Hassain would soon recover to give the alarm. Veronica still feared that she might have killed him, but she had not made sure and Roger felt instinctively that that was too much to hope for.

There were still movements around the camp fires along the front of the rebel stronghold, but holding firmly on to Veronica with one hand and gripping his newly-acquired rifle in the other, Roger stole quietly away towards the rear of the encampment. He was tempted strongly to go in search of the Egyptian Major and finish him off permanently with the stolen knife that was now stuck into the belt at his waist, but that would have meant risking recapture, and as he still had Veronica to consider he pushed the thought aside.

They moved like stealthy ghosts through the empty shells of the ruined village, skulking through the patches of greater darkness as they made for the dead end walls of the wide ravine. There were no guards here, for this way there was neither exit nor entry, and once they reached the cliff face they stopped to reconnoitre their position.

They felt momentarily safe against the pitch blackness of the cliff, and below them down the slight sandy slope they had a clear view of the nest of rebels that they had left. They could just see over the broken walls to the tents and camp fires, and so far there were no signs of any pursuit.

Behind them was the dead end, and their only way was to edge forwards along the cliff and work their way past the encampment below. Farther ahead, where the ravine narrowed towards its outlet, Roger guessed that there would be sentries, but he could only hope that they would be beyond the cave that formed the ammunition dump, and that once he had blown that up he and Veronica could escape in the confusion.

They moved silently with their backs to the wall, either stepping around rocks or climbing over them. Roger had released Veronica and now gripped his rifle with both hands but she stuck close behind him.

For ten minutes they made slow, stealthy progress, working their way past the lair of the Red Wolves and feeling cautiously for footholds in the darkness. The slope below was not exceptionally steep, but to have kicked a scattering of boulders down it could well have caused them disaster. Still there was no outcry from below, and Roger was beginning to feel that they really had a chance. And then he saw the alert outline of a sentry just ahead.

The man had already seen them and it was too late to step back. The shadowy figure was already twisting in an effort to bring his rifle to bear, but before he could fire Roger had closed with him in a savage rush. Roger's own rifle swept up in a violent arc and the butt cracked squarely under the tribesman's chin. The man spun round as though his head had been flicked sideways with a whip and toppled headlong to the sand.

Roger stood over the man, breathing hard and with Veronica pressing close behind him, and slowly he realized that they were directly in front of the large cave. He had not noticed it before for the entrance was barely visible against the overall blackness of the cliffs, and with a deep sense of relief he realized that he had already dealt with the only guard.

The feeling vanished as they heard the first clamour of alarm from below. Veronica stared white-faced down the slope and then Roger grabbed at her arm.

"Quickly," he hissed. "They've missed us and we can't have much time."

He hustled her desperately into the stygian blackness of the cave mouth and slung the rifle over his shoulder by its strap. They felt their way inside until they were clear of the entrance, groping along the harsh, rock walls, and then Roger fumbled in his pocket for his cigarette lighter. He flicked it on, and in the light of the tiny, wavering flame they looked slowly around them.

The cave was about ten feet wide and ten feet high, running back for perhaps thirty yards. In the centre, about half way back from the entrance were stacks of heavy boxes all piled together. Roger swiftly gave Veronica the lighter and then moved towards them. He pulled his knife from his belt, and alternately using the wide blade and the barrel of his rifle he splintered open the top boards of several of the long crates and levered them up. The first two crates were filled with packed rounds of ammunition, but the third was full of what looked like four-inch metal pineapples which he knew were Mills bombs.

Roger lifted two of the ugly little brutes from their nesting places and said softly.

"These should do it. We'll chuck them behind us as we leave, and if that doesn't create one hell of a bang then I'll come back and eat what's left."

Veronica nodded and flicked off the lighter. Total darkness engulfed them once more, and she held on to his arm as they made their way gingerly to the cave entrance. When they reached it they heard an increased pandemonium of shouts and rushing movement taking place below, but Roger ignored it and pushed Veronica away from him.

"Start running," he hissed. "I'll be right behind you."

Veronica nodded and moved away. She hurried along the cliff face and then turned to wait for him. She could just distinguish his kneeling shape as he crouched in the cave mouth and she saw him fumble with the bombs as he removed the pins. He bowled them fast into the cave with swift underarm

361

movements, and then he straightened up and ran to join her. In the same instant she saw the dark figure looming behind him.

Even in the night there was no mistaking their enemy, for Faizal Hassain was still stripped to the waist, and the blood where she had struck him down still glistened wetly on his thin, tight-mouthed face. She saw the levelled revolver in his hand as he ran forward, and desperately she screamed a warning.

"Roger, behind you!"

Roger made a frantic effort to twist round in full flight and tumbled headlong as he missed his footing. He rolled on to his back on the sand and fumbled clumsily to untangle his rifle from his shoulder. Hassain had stopped dead as he saw his quarry fall and he laughed at the muddling mess that the young Englishman was making, and calmly he lowered the aim of his revolver.

He delayed a fraction too late for in that instant the two Mills bombs blew up with a shattering crump, and almost in the same moment came a further series of deafening explosions as the rest of the stored ammunition followed suit. A blast of fire ripped out of the cave mouth, almost enveloping the horrified Egyptian who was standing full in its path, and then it seemed that hundreds of rounds of high velocity bullets were ricocheting off the walls of the cave and speeding outwards through the only exit. Hassain shrieked as his body was flung aside, smashed by fire and bullets as it slithered down the slope towards the camp fires of the Red Wolves.

Roger and Veronica scrambled towards each other, meeting and holding themselves desperately upright as fire and smoke continued to belch from the depths of the cave. There was no doubt that this time the Egyptian Major was dead, but after a moment Roger said.

"We must move, Ronnie. The sound of that little lot should have carried to that patrol, but it won't help us very much if the Red Wolves catch up with us first."

She nodded and they began to hurry away along the ravine. They stayed with the cliff wall where the darkness hid them and Roger carried the rifle at the ready. Once they had to crouch low among some broken rocks that had fallen from the cliff face, as two men rushed below them in the night. The men were running from the ravine entrance towards the encampment, and Roger realized that they must be the sentries who would obviously have been posted. He was very glad that they had panicked, and seizing Veronica's arm he too began to run, but in the opposite direction.

They knew that their lives now depended upon speed and so they ran as never before. Behind them there was still uproar and shouted curses, but mercifully there was no real pursuit. They reached the end of the ravine and Roger heaved a sigh of relief now that they were at last able to turn away up the mountainside. They had placed a good mile between themselves and the Red Wolves, and as they were both stumbling from exhaustion he considered that it was time they found somewhere to hide.

Fortunately the mountainside was well provided with slopes of jumbled rock, and they had no difficulty in concealing themselves in a small crevice. An overhanging slab of rock shut out the stars and they huddled together wearily in the darkness, spending a sleepless night with the rifle constantly at the ready.

Their worst moment came when they heard the hurried sounds of men and camels passing below. They listened to the sounds with thudding hearts, but then Roger realized that the tribesmen were not organizing a search but were hastily clearing out. Now that their ammunition dump had been destroyed they had nothing to protect, and they too had realized that the explosion would be sure to attract the attention of the lurking British patrol if it were still within hearing. No doubt they would return to search these hillsides in daylight if the patrol failed to show up, but meanwhile they were playing safe.

For the rest of the night Roger and Veronica lay in each other's arms with the rifle almost between them. Their fate was still uncertain, and their eyes were tired and puffy when daylight at last began to brighten the bleak mountainside.

They crawled from their hiding place, stretching cramped limbs and staring dully at the wilderness around them. Dawn in the Radfan Mountains was a sight to be enjoyed, but they were impressed only by the harsh emptiness of the peaks. They might have been alone on the mountains of Mars, and Veronica shuddered a little as she stood close against Roger's side.

They kept their heads low, for Roger did not trust this hostile world, and he was not at all sure that the Red Wolves had vanished so completely. And then after half an hour they heard the longed-for sound of approaching vehicles.

They watched as three fast armoured cars jolted up the rock-strewn floor of the valley that led to the narrower ravine from which they had only just escaped, and both of them felt weak with relief. Their feelings were equal to those when the *Judith Rose* had picked them up from the Red Sea and they both stood upright and waved wildly.

In the leading Scout car an astonished

Lieutenant slowly raised his hand to halt his patrol. The men under his command tightened their hands on submachine guns and automatic rifles as they saw that one of the waving figures was armed, but when they saw that he was running down the slope to meet them and that his companion was a woman they held their fire.

The young Lieutenant went half way to meet them, and although he looked very tough and capable his eyes still held frank amazement. He said helplessly.

"And who the devil might you be?"

Roger grinned at him and said wearily. "My name is Stewart. Roger Stewart. And this is my wife Veronica." He tightened his arm around her and added somewhat inanely. "How do you do?"

"Very well, thank you." The Lieutenant blinked and then said hastily. "But this is ridiculous! What the devil are you doing out here?"

Roger smiled at him. "You may not believe it, but we're supposed to be on our honeymoon. Although after you've taken us back to Aden and they've flown us home to England, we're going to finish it at dear old dull, respectable Brighton!"

And all the Lieutenant could say was, "Ye Gods!" And shake his head in wonderment.

THE END

Other titles in the
Linford Mystery Library:

A GENTEEL LITTLE MURDER
Philip Daniels

Gilbert had a long-cherished plan to murder his wife. When the polished Edward entered the scene Gilbert's attitude was suddenly changed.

DEATH AT THE WEDDING
Madelaine Duke

Dr. Norah North's search for a killer takes her from a wedding to a private hospital.

MURDER FIRST CLASS
Ron Ellis

Will Detective Chief Inspector Glass find the Post Office robbers before the Executioner gets to them?

A FOOT IN THE GRAVE
Bruce Marshall

About to be imprisoned and tortured in Buenos Aires, John Smith escapes, only to become involved in an aeroplane hijacking.

DEAD TROUBLE
Martin Carroll

Trespassing brought Jennifer Denning more than she bargained for. She was totally unprepared for the violence which was to lie in her path.

HOURS TO KILL
Ursula Curtiss

Margaret went to New Mexico to look after her sick sister's rented house and felt a sharp edge of fear when the absent landlady arrived.

THE DEATH OF ABBE DIDIER
Richard Grayson

Inspector Gautier of the Sûreté investigates three crimes which are strangely connected.

NIGHTMARE TIME
Hugh Pentecost

Have the missing major and his wife met with foul play somewhere in the Beaumont Hotel, or is their disappearance a carefully planned step in an act of treason?

BLOOD WILL OUT
Margaret Carr

Why was the manor house so oddly familiar to Elinor Howard? Who would have guessed that a Sunday School outing could lead to murder?

THE DRACULA MURDERS
Philip Daniels

The Horror Ball was interrupted by a spectral figure who warned the merrymakers they were tampering with the unknown.

THE LADIES
OF LAMBTON GREEN
Liza Shepherd

Why did murdered Robin Colquhoun's picture pose such a threat to the ladies of Lambton Green?

CARNABY
AND THE GAOLBREAKERS
Peter N. Walker

Detective Sergeant James Aloysius Carnaby-King is sent to prison as bait. When he joins in an escape he is thrown headfirst into a vicious murder hunt.

MUD IN HIS EYE
Gerald Hammond

The harbourmaster's body is found mangled beneath Major Smyle's yacht. What is the sinister significance of the illicit oysters?

THE SCAVENGERS
Bill Knox

Among the masses of struggling fish in the *Tecta's* nets was a larger, darker, ominously motionless form . . . the body of a skin diver.

DEATH IN ARCADY
Stella Phillips

Detective Inspector Matthew Furnival works unofficially with the local police when a brutal murder takes place in a caravan camp.

STORM CENTRE
Douglas Clark

Detective Chief Superintendent Masters, temporarily lecturing in a police staff college, finds there's more to the job than a few weeks relaxation in a rural setting.

THE MANUSCRIPT MURDERS
Roy Harley Lewis

Antiquarian bookseller Matthew Coll, acquires a rare 16th century manuscript. But when the Dutch professor who had discovered the journal is murdered, Coll begins to doubt its authenticity.

SHARENDEL
Margaret Carr

Ruth didn't want all that money. And she didn't want Aunt Cass to die. But at Sharendel things looked different. She began to wonder if she had a split personality.

MURDER TO BURN
Laurie Mantell

Sergeants Steven Arrow and Lance Brendon, of the New Zealand police force, come upon a woman's body in the water. When the dead woman is identified they begin to realise that they are investigating a complex fraud.

YOU CAN HELP ME
Maisie Birmingham

Whilst running the Citizens' Advice Bureau, Kate Weatherley is attacked with no apparent motive. Then the body of one of her clients is found in her room.

DAGGERS DRAWN
Margaret Carr

Stacey Manston was the kind of girl who could take most things in her stride, but three murders were something different . . .

THE MONTMARTRE MURDERS
Richard Grayson

Inspector Gautier of Sûreté investigates the disappearance of artist Théo, the heir to a fortune.

GRIZZLY TRAIL
Gwen Moffat

Miss Pink, alone in the Rockies, helps in a search for missing hikers, solves two cruel murders and has the most terrifying experience of her life when she meets a grizzly bear!

BLINDMAN'S BLUFF
Margaret Carr

Kate Deverill had considered suicide. It was one way out — and preferable to being murdered.

BEGOTTEN MURDER
Martin Carroll

When Susan Phillips joined her aunt on a voyage of 12,000 miles from her home in Melbourne, she little knew their arrival would germinate the seeds of murder planted long ago.

WHO'S THE TARGET?
Margaret Carr

Three people whom Abby could identify as her parents' murderers wanted her dead, but she decided that maybe Jason could have been the target.

THE LOOSE SCREW
Gerald Hammond

After a motor smash, Beau Pepys and his cousin Jacqueline, her fiancé and dotty mother, suspect that someone had prearranged the death of their friend. But who, and why?

CASE WITH THREE HUSBANDS
Margaret Erskine

Was it a ghost of one of Rose Bonner's late husbands that gave her old Aunt Agatha such a terrible shock and then murdered her in her bed?

THE END OF THE RUNNING
Alan Evans

Lang continued to push the men and children on and on. Behind them were the men who were hunting them down, waiting for the first signs of exhaustion before they pounced.

CARNABY AND THE HIJACKERS
Peter N. Walker

When Commander Pigeon assigns Detective Sergeant Carnaby-King to prevent a raid on a bullion-carrying passenger train, he knows that there are traitors in high positions.